FLOWERS FOR THE BROKEN

FLOWERS FOR THE BROKEN

Stories by
Benjamin Alire Sáenz

Broken Moon Press • Seattle

Printed in the United States of America.
ISBN 0-913089-28-1
Library of Congress Catalog Card Number: 92-70017

Cover image, "Flowers for the Broken," copyright © 1990
by Patricia Ridenour. Used by permission of the photographer. Author photo copyright © 1991 by Amy Dawson.
Used by permission of the photographer.

Thanks to the editors and publishers of the following
journals, where some of these stories first appeared,
in earlier versions: "Alligator Park" in *The Fifteenth
Annual Chicano Literary Awards* (University of
California, Irvine), "Cebolleros" in *Saguaro*, "Exiled"
in *The Rio Grande Review* and *The Texas Observer*
(under a different title), "Flowers for the Broken"
in *Blue Mesa Review*, "Holy Week" in *Imagine: An
International Journal of Chicano Poetry* (Special Fiction
Issue), and "A Silent Love" in *The Guadalupe Review*.

Editor: Mary Helen Clarke
Copy editors: Cathy A. Johnson
               and Lesley Link
Proofreader: Cathy A. Johnson

Broken Moon Press
Post Office Box 24585
Seattle, Washington 98124-0585 USA

For the voices of my people
who have given me my heart,

and for
my mother and father,
my brothers and sisters,
my nephews and nieces,

and for Barbara

CONTENTS

ACKNOWLEDGMENTS

These stories were written over a period of six years—in different cities—in different states (emotional and geographical): Texas, New Mexico, Iowa, California. I was lucky enough to have encountered some very fine people along the way. I'd like to thank a few of them who inspired these stories—or helped me write them—or just plain helped me when I was in need. Teresa Melendez-Hayes and Ricardo Aguilar (who were the first to read my stories and encourage me), Barbara DuMond and Virginia Navarro (who were there when I began writing—who have always been there), Garrett Lowe Mullen (yes, there's life after Iowa City), Denise Levertov (where she lives, there's always room at the inn), Arturo Islas (Rest in Peace, Arturo—I miss you), Stacey Vallas (is there a Rudy's in heaven?), and Amy Dawson (who wanted all the stories she read to be novels—maybe in the next life, Amy). Special thanks to Karen Fiser (such a fine human being, and smart, too: she dreams of living in New Mexico), Lawrence J. Schmidt (a real mensch—I never tire of thanking this guy), John Ellison and Lesley Link (good publishers and good people). And hats off (let's make it a Stetson) to Mary Helen Clarke—a wonderful editor. *Mil Gracias*.

EXILE EL PASO, TEXAS

[PROLOGUE]

That morning—when the day was new, when the sun slowly touched the sky, almost afraid to break it—that morning I looked out my window and stared at the Juárez Mountains. Mexican purples—burning. I had always thought of them as sacraments of belonging. That was the first time it happened. It had happened to others, but it had never happened to me. And when it happened, it started a fire, a fire that will burn for a long time.

As I walked to school, I remember thinking what a perfect place Sunset Heights was: turn of the century houses intact; remodeled houses painted pink and turquoise; old homes tastefully gentrified by the aspiring young; the rundown Sunset Grocery store decorated with the protest art of graffiti on one end and a plastic-signed "Circle K" on the other.

This was the edge of the piece of paper that was America, the border that bordered the University—its buildings, its libraries; the border that bordered the freeway—its cars coming and going, coming and going endlessly; the border that bordered downtown—its banks and businesses and bars; the border that bordered the border between two countries.

The unemployed poor from Juárez knocking on doors and asking for jobs—or money—or food. Small parks filled with people whose English did not exist. The upwardly mobile living next to families whose only concern was getting enough money to pay next month's rent. Some had lived here for generations, would continue living here into the next century; others would live here a few days. All this color, all this color, all this color beneath the shadow of the Juárez Mountains. Sunset Heights: a perfect place with a perfect name, and a perfect view of the river.

After class, I went by my office and drank a cup of coffee, sat and read, and did some writing. It was a quiet day on campus, nothing but me and my work—the kind of day the mind needs to catch up with itself, the kind of uneventful day so necessary for living. I started walking home at about three o'clock, after I had put my things together in my torn backpack. I made a mental note to sew the damn thing. *One day everything's gonna come tumbling out—better sew it.* I'd made that mental note before.

Walking down Prospect, I thought maybe I'd go for a jog. I hoped the spring would not bring too much wind this year. The wind, common desert rain; the wind blew too hard and harsh sometimes; the wind unsettled the desert—upset things, ruined the calmness of the spring. My mind wandered, searched the black asphalt littered with torn papers; the chained dogs in the yards who couldn't hurt me; the even bricks of all the houses I passed. I belonged here, yes. I belonged. Thoughts entered like children running through a park. This year, maybe the winds would not come.

I didn't notice the green car drive up and stop right next to me as I walked. The border patrol interrupted my daydreaming: "Where are you from?"

I didn't answer. I wasn't sure who the agent, a woman, was addressing.

She repeated the question in Spanish, *"¿De dónde eres?"*

Without thinking, I almost answered her question—in Spanish. A reflex. I caught myself in midsentence and stuttered in a nonlanguage.

"¿Dónde naciste?" she asked again.

By then my mind had cleared, and quietly I said: "I'm a U.S. citizen."

"Were you born in the United States?"

She was browner than I was. I might have asked her the same question. I looked at her for awhile—searching for something I recognized.

"Yes," I answered.

"Where in the United States were you born?"

"In New Mexico."

"Where in New Mexico?"

"Las Cruces."

"What do you do?"

"I'm a student."

"And are you employed?"

"Sort of."

"Sort of?" She didn't like my answer. Her tone bordered on anger. I looked at her expression and decided it wasn't hurting anyone to answer her questions. It was all very innocent, just a game we were playing.

"I work at the University as a teaching assistant."

She didn't respond. She looked at me as if I were a blank. Her eyes were filling in the empty spaces as she looked at my face. I looked at her for a second and decided she was finished with me. I started walking away. "Are you sure you were born in Las Cruces?" she asked again.

I turned around and smiled, "Yes, I'm sure." She didn't smile back. She and the driver sat there for awhile and watched me as I continued walking. They drove past me slowly and then proceeded down the street.

I didn't much care for the color of their cars.

"Sons of bitches," I whispered, "pretty soon I'll have to carry a passport in my own neighborhood." I said it to be flippant; something in me rebelled against people dressed in uniforms. I wasn't angry—not then, not at first, not really angry. In less than ten minutes I was back in my apartment playing the scene again and again in my mind. It was like a video I played over and over—memorizing the images. Something was wrong. I was embarrassed, ashamed because I'd been so damned compliant like a piece of tin foil in the uniformed woman's hand. Just like a child in the principal's office, in trouble for speaking Spanish. "I should have told that witch exactly what I thought of her and her green car and her green uniform."

I lit a cigarette and told myself I was overreacting. "Breathe in—breathe out—breathe in—breathe out—no big deal—you live on a border. These things happen—just one of those things. Just a game…" I changed into my jogging clothes and went for a run. At the top of the hill on Sunbowl Drive, I stopped to stare at the Juárez Mountains. I felt the sweat run down my face. I kept running until I could no longer hear *Are you sure you were born in Las Cruces?* ringing in my ears.

《 》

School let out in early May. I spent the last two weeks of that month relaxing and working on some paintings. In June I got back to working on my stories. I had a working title, which I hated, but I hated it less than the actual stories I was writing. It would come to nothing; I knew it

xiv   Flowers for the Broken

would come to nothing.

From my window I could see the freeway. It was then I realized that not a day went by when I didn't see someone running across the freeway or walking down the street looking out for someone. They were people who looked not so different from me—except that they lived their lives looking over their shoulders.

One Thursday, I saw the border patrol throw some men into their van—throw them—as if they were born to be thrown like baseballs, like rings in a carnival ringtoss, easy inanimate objects, dead bucks after a deer hunt. The illegals didn't even put up a fight. They were aliens, from somewhere else, somewhere foreign, and it did not matter that the "somewhere else" was as close as an eyelash to an eye. What mattered was that someone had once drawn a line, and once drawn, that line became indelible and hard and could not be crossed.

The men hung their heads so low that they almost scraped the littered asphalt. Whatever they felt, they did not show; whatever burned did not burn for an audience. I sat at my typewriter and tried to pretend I saw nothing. *What do you think happens when you peer out windows? Buy curtains.*

I didn't write the rest of the day. I kept seeing the border patrol woman against a blue sky turning green. I thought of rearranging my desk so I wouldn't be next to the window, but I thought of the mountains. No, I would keep my desk near the window, but I would look only at the mountains.

<< >>

Two weeks later, I went for a walk. The stories weren't going well that day; my writing was getting worse instead of better; my characters were getting on my nerves—I didn't like them—no one else would like them either. They did not burn with anything. I hadn't showered, hadn't shaved, hadn't combed my hair. I threw some water on my face and walked out the door. It was summer; it was hot; it was afternoon, the time of day when everything felt as if it were on fire. The worst time of the day to take a walk. I wiped the sweat from my eyelids; it instantly reappeared. I wiped it off again, but the sweat came pouring out—a leak in the dam. Let it leak. I laughed. A hundred degrees in the middle of a desert afternoon. Laughter poured out of me as fast as my sweat. I turned the corner and headed back home. I saw the green van. It was parked right ahead of me.

A man about my height got out of the van and approached me. Another man, taller, followed him. *"¿Tienes tus papeles?"* he asked. His gringo accent was as thick as the sweat on my skin.

"I can speak English," I said. I started to add: *I can probably speak it better than you,* but I stopped myself. No need to be aggressive, no need to get any hotter.

"Do you live in this neighborhood?"

"Yes."

"Where?"

"Down the street."

"Where down the street?"

"Are you planning on making a social visit?"

He gave me a hard look—cold and blue—then looked at his partner. He didn't like me. I didn't care. I liked that he hated me. It made it easier.

I watched them drive away and felt as hot as the air, felt as hot as the heat that was burning away the blue in the sky.

There were other times when I felt watched. Sometimes, when I jogged, the green vans would slow down, eye me. I felt like prey, like a rabbit who smelled the hunter. I pretended not to notice them. I stopped pretending. I started noting their presence in our neighborhood more and more. I started growing suspicious of my own observations. Of course, they weren't everywhere. But they *were* everywhere. I had just been oblivious to their presence, had been oblivious because they had nothing to do with me; their presence had something to do with someone else. I was not a part of this. I wanted no part of it. The green cars and the green vans clashed with the purples of the Juárez Mountains. Nothing looked the same. I never talked about their presence to other people. Sometimes the topic of the *Migra* would come up in conversations. I felt the burning; I felt the anger, would control it. I casually referred to them as the Gestapo, the traces of rage carefully hidden from the expression on my face—and everyone would laugh. I hated them.

When school started in the fall, I was stopped again. Again I had been walking home from the University. I heard the familiar question: "Where are you from?"

"Leave me alone."

"Are you a citizen of the United States?"

"Yes."

"Can you prove it?"

"No. No, I can't."

He looked at my clothes: jeans, tennis shoes, and a casual California shirt. He noticed my backpack full of books.

"You a student?"

I nodded and stared at him.

"There isn't any need to be unfriendly—"

"I'd like you to leave me alone."

"Just doing my job," he laughed. I didn't smile back. *Terrorists. Nazis did their jobs. Death squads in El Salvador and Guatemala did their jobs, too.* An unfair analogy. An unfair analogy? Yes, unfair. I thought it; I felt it; it was no longer my job to excuse—someone else would have to do that, someone else. The Juárez Mountains did not seem purple that fall. They no longer burned with color.

In early January I went with Michael to Juárez. Michael was from New York, and he had come to work in a home for the homeless in South El Paso. We weren't in Juárez very long—just looking around and getting gas. Gas was cheap in Juárez. On the way back, the customs officer asked us to declare our citizenship. "U.S. citizen," I said. "U.S. citizen," Michael followed. The customs officer lowered his head and poked it in the car. "What are you bringing over?"

"Nothing."

He looked at me. "Where in the United States were you born?"

"In Las Cruces, New Mexico."

He looked at me a while longer. "Go ahead," he signaled.

I noticed that he didn't ask Michael where he was from. But Michael had blue eyes; Michael had white skin. Michael didn't have to tell the man in the uniform where he was from.

≪ ≫

That winter, Sunset Heights seemed deserted to me. The streets were empty like the river. One morning, I was driving down Upson Street toward the University, the wind shaking the limbs of the bare trees. Nothing to shield them—unprotected by green leaves. The sun burned a dull yellow. In front of me, I noticed two border patrol officers chasing someone, though that someone was not visible. One of them put his hand out, signaling me to slow down as they ran across the street in front of my car. They were running with their billy clubs in hand. The wind blew at their backs as if to urge them on, as if to carry them.

In late January, Michael and I went to Juárez again. A friend of his was in town, and he wanted to see Juárez. We walked across the bridge, across the river, across the line into another country. It was easy. No one there to stop us. We walked the streets of Juárez, streets that had seen better years, that were tired now from the tired feet that walked them. Michael's friend wanted to know how it was that there were so many beggars. "Were there always so many? Has it always been this way?" I didn't know how it had always been. We sat in the Cathedral and in the old chapel next to it and watched people rubbing the feet of statues; when I touched a statue, it was warmer than my own hand. We walked to the marketplace and inhaled the smells. Grocery stores in the country we knew did not have such smells. On the way back we stopped in a small bar and had a beer. The beer was cold and cheap. Walking back over the bridge, we stopped at the top and looked out at the city of El Paso. "It actually looks pretty from here, doesn't it?" I said. Michael nodded. It did look pretty. We looked off to the side—down the river—and for a long time watched the people trying to get across. Michael's friend said it was like watching *The CBS Evening News.*

As we reached the customs building, we noticed that a border patrol van pulled up behind the building where the other green cars were parked. The officers jumped out of the van and threw a handcuffed man against one of the parked cars. It looked like they were going to beat him. Two more border patrol officers pulled up in a car and jumped out to join them. One of the officers noticed we were watching. They straightened the man out and walked him inside—like gentlemen. They would have beat him. They would have beat him. But we were watching.

My fingers wanted to reach through the wire fence, not to touch it, not to feel it, but to break it down, to melt it down with what I did not understand. The burning was not there to be understood. Something was burning, the side of me that knew I was treated different, would always be treated different because I was born on a particular side of a fence, a fence that separated me from others, that separated me from a past, that separated me from the country of my genesis and glued me to the country I did not love because it demanded something of me I could not give. Something was burning now, and if I could have grasped the source of that rage and held it in my fist, I would have melted that fence. Someone built that fence; someone could tear it down. Maybe I could tear it down; maybe I was the one. Maybe then I would no longer be separated.

« »

The first day in February, I was walking to a downtown Chevron station to pick up my car. On the corner of Prospect and Upson, a green car was parked—just sitting there. A part of my landscape. I was walking on the opposite side of the street. For some reason, I knew they were going to stop me. My heart clenched like a fist; the muscles in my back knotted up. *Maybe they'll leave me alone. I should have taken a shower this morning. I should have worn a nicer sweater. I should have put on a pair of socks, worn a nicer pair of shoes. I should have cut my hair; I should have shaved…*

The driver rolled down his window. I saw him from the corner of my eye. He called me over to him—*whistled me over*—much like he'd call a dog. I kept walking. He whistled me over again. *Here, boy.* I stopped for a second. Only a second. I kept walking. The border patrol officer and a policeman rushed out of the car and ran toward me. I was sure they were going to tackle me, drag me to the ground, handcuff me. They stopped in front of me.

"Can I see your driver's license?" the policeman asked.

"Since when do you need a driver's license to walk down the street?" Our eyes met. "Did I do something against the law?"

The policeman was annoyed. He wanted me to be passive, to say: "Yes, sir." He wanted me to approve of his job.

"Don't you know what we do?"

"Yes, I know what you do."

"Don't give me a hard time. I don't want trouble. I just want to see some identification."

I looked at him—looked, and saw what would not go away: neither him, nor his car, nor his job, nor what I knew, nor what I felt. He stared back. He hated me as much as I hated him. He saw the bulge of my cigarettes under my sweater and crumpled them.

I backed away from his touch. "I smoke. It's not good for me, but it's not against the law. Not yet, anyway. Don't touch me. I don't like that. Read me my rights, throw me in the can, or leave me alone." I smiled.

"No one's charging you with anything."

My eyes followed them as they walked back to their car. Now it was war, and *I had won this battle*. Had I won this battle? Had I won?

« »

This spring morning, I sit at my desk, wait for the coffee to brew, and look out my window. This day, like every day, I look out my window. Across the street, a border patrol van stops and an officer gets out. So close I could touch him. On the freeway—this side of the river—a man is running. I put on my glasses. I am afraid he will be run over by the cars. I cheer for him. *Be careful. Don't get run over.* So close to the other side he can touch it. The border patrol officer gets out his walkie-talkie and runs toward the man who has disappeared from my view. I go and get my cup of coffee. I take a drink—slowly, it mixes with yesterday's tastes in my mouth. The officer in the green uniform comes back into view. He has the man with him. He puts him in the van. I can't see the color in their eyes. I see only the green. They drive away. There is no trace that says they've been there. The mountains watch the scene and say nothing. The mountains, ablaze in the spring light, have been watching—and guarding—and keeping silent longer than I have been alive. They will continue their vigil long after I am dead.

The green vans. They are taking someone away. They are taking. Green vans. This is my home, I tell myself. But I am not sure if I want this to be my home anymore. The thought crosses my mind to walk out of my apartment without my wallet. The thought crosses my mind that maybe the *Migra* will stop me again. I will let them arrest me. I will let them warehouse me. I will let them push me in front of a judge who will look at me like he has looked at the millions before me. I will be sent back to Mexico. I will let them treat me like I am illegal. But the thoughts pass. I am not brave enough to let them do that to me.

Today, the spring winds blow outside my window. The reflections in the pane, graffiti burning questions into the glass: *Sure you were born…Identification…Do you live?…* The winds will unsettle the desert—cover Sunset Heights with green dust. The vans will stay in my mind forever. I cannot banish them. I cannot banish their questions: *Where are you from?* I no longer know.

This is a true story.

"There are a lot of us around whose capacity
to love has been damaged..."

EDUARDO GALEANO

FLOWERS FOR THE BROKEN

CEBOLLEROS

«1959»

The little boy and his father walked out of the barber shop on Picacho Street into the light of a summer evening. The boy thought the shadows were alive, speaking to him, whispering in his ears. He stared at the faded blues and reds of the barbershop pole winding forever down. The street was quiet, and the passing cars said things to the street, secrets the boy wanted to know, to touch. And for a moment, he imagined he was a car with tires talking to the streets in a language only the asphalt and the shadows understood.

The west side of town was dying. The hotels, peeling like sun-burned skin, no longer attracted overnight tourists on their way to California. Music floated out of the rooms, music, Mexican music, from another country. The boy liked the music, and he tapped his foot to the rhythm and heard his mother singing as she did the laundry. Somewhere inside of him she was smiling. He wanted to dance but didn't know how. No one had ever taught him. He was a tire; he was dancing on the street to the music, the Mexican music, and the street melted with his secrets. The shadows of the evening were dreaming of another country, and the boy was the heart of the country, a new country.

An old truck with the same sunburned skin as the hotels drove slowly down the street. The truck had a long bed full of migrants and a railing; the people looked as if they were surrounded by a fence. They were colored in sweat, shiny and smooth, and their smell mingled with the shadows and the onions they picked. Early evening air and summer onions. The boy wanted to know, wanted to be the sweat and the smells, wanted to be the deep blue in the sky that would be turning pink and orange in a matter of minutes, wanted to be the magic.

"¡Cebolleros!" his father yelled as the truck drove past them. His

voice was deep and harsh. He laughed and yelled it again. *"¡Cebolleros!"* The sound echoed in the boy's ears. Cebolleros. Cebolleros. The boy stared up at his father's moustache. He didn't like the sound of the words, but the people didn't seem to mind. He watched the people in the truck, and his eyes caught the face of a sunbrowned woman who smiled at him. He wanted to ask his father why the people were fenced in, but his father didn't like questions. The boy looked at his father's moustache and then smiled back at the woman. She blew him a soft kiss and laughed.

The truck came to a complete stop. The boy stared at the tires and wanted to be the truck. If he were the truck he would let the people out of the fence. Some of the men jumped off the truck holding their sweaty shirts in their hands. The boy stared at the shirtless men, the muscles, the strong backs. Maybe someday he would be strong like them. The men were laughing and saying things to each other: *"Ahora si, unas cuantas cervecitas."* The men laughed and went inside the hotel where the music was coming from. The little boy knew they were going inside to dance because they seemed happy. He glanced at the woman who had thrown him a kiss. He wanted to tell her she was good and beautiful. He couldn't take his eyes off her. *"¡Cebolleros!"* his father yelled again. The little boy didn't like the sound of it.

The truck drove away, the truck with the woman and the people and the fence around them. The boy watched them all disappear. "I wish I were a truck," he whispered. *"Pobres pendejos,"* his father said. The boy looked up at his father and wondered what he would look like without his moustache. When he grew up, he didn't want to have hair growing over *his* lip.

«1967»

My father lost his job that spring. That was the way of the construction business. That spring, no one was building. I heard my parents talking in the kitchen. I could hear them always—I could hear everything from everywhere. No one had any secrets. I was sitting in our room trying to read a book. I used to get lost in books, but that evening I wasn't lost. My parents were talking about what had to be done. The money my mother was making at the factory where she inspected pantyhose wasn't enough. It wouldn't be much of a summer without money. No swimming, no movies. No money, no summer. "I'll have to keep looking," my father said, *"tiene que haber trabajo."* And then he said that my older brother had to find a job to help out. I tried to imagine my brother working, the brother I always fought with, the brother who slept in the same bed I did, my brother who was only one year older than me. Fifteen wasn't old enough to get a job. "He's too young," I heard my mother say, *"no quiero que se salga a trabajar tan joven."*

"He can lie about his age," my father said. But I knew no one would believe he was old enough to work. He couldn't even grow a moustache. After a long silence my father said there might not be a job for him anyway, maybe a job for no one.

I heard my two younger brothers arguing over what they should watch on television. They were always fighting, but they were always happy. School would be out in another week. They would laugh and fight all summer. I walked out of our room and told them both to stop arguing or I'd turn off the television. They made faces at me—then laughed. Julian, the youngest, told me he wanted a television that showed things in color. "Just pretend," I told him. "it's more fun that way." I walked into the kitchen where my parents were drinking coffee. My father kept combing his hair with his fingers, always working. He had big hands, rough, strong like his voice. I stared at his moustache that covered his whole face. I wanted to say something but didn't know what, so I said nothing. I looked at my mother and smiled. She smiled back—we had secrets. I remember that spring.

There wasn't much to do after school let out. My father was home all the time, so we had to ask him for permission to do everything. It was better when he was working—when he was working, we could go anywhere we wanted. We couldn't even have a good fight because it made my father nervous. My brother and I kept wishing Dad would find a job before everyone exploded.

I was always reading books. Library books; long books about English people, novels about men and women falling in love in London or in the country. I remember thinking that where they lived was not like New Mexico. It was green, not like the desert. I imagined their rivers were blue, and they probably had boats, and the people in all those books didn't need to work. But I knew they were just books, and people didn't want to read books about people's work—so they kept the work out of it. I kept an eye on my younger brothers as I read, and every day it was my job to make lunch. Mostly I warmed up the food my mother left for us. My father was very quiet when we ate.

After two weeks, I heard my father tell my mother that we were going to pick onions. "Not much pay," he said, *"pero siquiera no me vuelvo loco."* That Sunday, my father told us that the onions were ready. He had spoken to a man he knew, and the man told him to come to the fields. "We're all going," he said. My brother and I looked at each other, but said nothing. "The kids too?" my older brother asked. "They can't stay here," my father said, "there's no one to take care of them. They can help us out."

Monday morning, when it was still dark, my mother woke us up with her whispers. She sounded like the rain. Everyone was too sleepy to say anything at breakfast, so we sat and heard each other eat. I watched my mother make the burritos, watched her hands move quietly. I watched her wide-awake face and the lines around her eyes. I wondered what she was thinking.

My father came into the kitchen and said it was time to go to the fields. I thought of the fields in the book I was reading, green and full of trees, English trees. My father reminded me and my brother that this was serious business. "We're here to work—not play. *No anden jugando.*" We nodded and looked at each other. As we walked outside, the sky was already turning blue. The morning, cool and soft, reminded me of my grandfather. In the morning, his chocolate eyes had been almost blue, showing me everything I ever wanted to see.

My father had collected plastic buckets for the onions—empty five gallon paint buckets that had been washed out. I looked at the scissors and turned them over in my hands. "I don't know how to use them," I told my brother. "Dad will show us," he said, "it'll be easy." He thought everything was easy. To me everything seemed hard like the cement driveway my father had poured last year.

We reached the fields as the sun lifted itself into the sky, turning the sky dusty blue. The people in the fields, wearing reds and pinks and blues, began claiming their rows. My father claimed some rows, and we followed him. My younger brothers were excited, and they kept running up and down the rows like it was a playground. The onions had been turned up by a machine and were lying on the ground waiting to be picked up. The smell of earth and onions dug into my skin, and I wanted to be an onion. I wanted to be the earth.

Everyone was talking. No one spoke English. I liked the sound of Spanish—it made me happy like the songs of my grandfather. My father went to talk to some of the men and then returned to the rows we had claimed and said we had to get to work. He looked at my brother and me and showed us how to clip the roots and the wilting tops. "We should have bought some gloves," he said, "but we can't be spending money on them right now. Maybe next week. You'll get blisters." He laughed. "It's all right, men's hands should have blisters."

I thought of the English novels where the men had no blisters on their hands, smooth, white hands—not like my father's. Dad rubbed my hair, and that made me smile. We got to work. I bent down and scooped up a smooth onion and cut it with my scissors, just the way my father had taught me. The snip sounded tinny as I cut the roots and the stems. Cutting. One onion, then another, then another. I was careful not to cut too close, because if I cut too close to the onion I'd ruin it, and we didn't get paid for ruining good onions. I watched myself cut the onions, cut them, and toss them carefully into my bucket until it was full. I pretended I was filling a basket with Easter eggs, yellow eggs, but it was hard to pretend because my hands were already getting blisters. The eggs were growing on my hands. "My hands are too soft," I mumbled, "they're not a man's hands." I stood straight, unbent my back, and showed my hands to my brother. He grinned and showed me his. Onions, yellow onions the color of my grandfather's teeth.

In the next row two women were talking as they worked. They were fast, much better than me and my brother. I thought of a man I had once seen drawing a church—he did it fast, perfect—perfect like the women in the next row. I heard them talking, voices like guitars singing serious songs: "Bueno, mi esposo es muy bueno pero toma mucho. Y mis hijos salieron peor. Dios mio, no se que voy hacer con esos hijos que tengo—pero son muy trabajadores."

My youngest brother came to take the bucket to empty it into a gunny sack. It was too heavy for him. I picked him up and threw him in the air—he was so small and happy. "Do it again," he yelled, "do it again." My other brother showed up, and together they carried the bucket of onions away. "This is fun," they yelled. But it wasn't. My back was beginning to feel bent and crooked. I arched myself as far back as I could—my neck stretching away from the ground. The woman in the next row smiled at me: "Que muchachito tan bonito." I bowed my head, bent my back toward the earth again—toward the earth and the onions.

By the end of the day I did not know how many sacks of onions we had picked. My brother asked my father. "Thirty," he said. Thirty, I thought, maybe a world record. My brother and I looked at each other and smiled. "Your nose is sunburned," my brother said. "So is yours." We fell to the ground wrestling and laughing. I heard my father talking to the men. They were laughing about something, too.

We walked back to my father's Studebaker, and my brother kept saying it was a dumb truck and that we needed a new one. He kept talking all the way home, but I wasn't listening. My nose was hurting; my back felt as if I had been carrying someone all day; my blisters were stinging. I wanted to go home and sleep. I didn't care how bad I smelled; I wanted to sleep or die or wake up in the fields of my novels. When we got home, my mother had dinner ready. She took my youngest brother in her arms and laughed. She looked so clean. She kissed me on the cheek and told me to take a shower.

I felt the hot water hit my body—I was a candle. I was melting into nothing. I ate the warm dinner but couldn't taste it. I was too tired to talk. My father told my mother we were going to have to work harder: "Only thirty sacks. *A viente y cinco centavos al costal nunca la vamos hacer.* Tomorrow we'll work harder."

I went to bed and did not read my English novel. My brother told me he was glad I wasn't going to read because he hated for the light to be on while he was trying to sleep. "You read too damn much anyway." I looked at him and wanted to stick my fist through his face. I threw my book across the room and turned off the light. I dreamed I had a horse and lived in a house where they played only Mexican music, a house where I could dance in every room.

The second day was the same as the first, only we worked harder, and wore hats. By the end of the day, we had picked fifty-five sacks. It was better, but it still wasn't enough. I dreamed I was standing on a hill made of onions. There was a huge crowd of English people yelling at me: "*¡Cebollero! ¡Cebollero!*" I woke up and smelled the onions and the dry earth. I walked into the bathroom and threw up. I didn't read any more books that summer.

The whole week was the same. We worked, we ate, we slept. The second week was better. I was getting used to the work, and we were up to seventy sacks of onions a day. I started hating the sun and the earth and the onions, but the voices of the people played over and over in my mind, the music. The music kept me working.

We moved to another field in the middle of the second week. When we left the old field I felt I was leaving something behind, but when I searched with my eyes, I saw nothing but graying earth and sacks of onions waiting to be picked up by other workers who would sort them. I half-thought that if I looked in each sack, I would find people hiding.

The first day of the third week was the same—until the afternoon. The sun was hotter than usual—white, blinding, everything feeling as if it were touched by flames. My father made sure we were drinking plenty of water. The afternoon was too hot for talking, and everyone worked quietly. In the silence all I could hear was the onions being dumped into gunny sacks and scissors snipping at roots and stems, but the sounds were distant—almost as if the sun were swallowing all the sounds we made with our work. The fields were strange. We were in another country, a country I didn't know.

"I'm an onion," I said out loud, "but I don't want to be one." My brother looked at me and told me I was saying dumb things. "If you say something like that one more time, I'm going to tell Dad you've had too much sun." "I am an onion," I said, "and so are you." He shook his head and kept working.

In the heat I heard a voice yelling, and some of the people working in the fields ran and hid in a nearby ditch. Other people just kept working. I didn't know why people were hiding, and the woman in the next row told me not to say anything to the *Migra*. *"Nomas no digas nada, mijo."* I nodded, but I wasn't sure what she was talking about. I was keeping a secret but I didn't know the secret. I looked at my brother and again I knew I was an onion.

The Border Patrol van stopped at the side of the road, and some men dressed in green uniforms got out and walked into the fields. They looked like soldiers. The men stopped and asked people questions. Some of the workers showed them pieces of paper and others showed them their wallets. One of the men in green came closer to our row. He asked the women in the row next to ours a strange question: *"¿Tienen papeles? ¿Permisos?"* I smiled at his Spanish, not like music, not even like a language. The women spoke to him in fragmented English. "I don't need paper," one woman told one of the men in green. Her voice was angry like a knife. She showed him a driver's license and what I thought was a birth certificate. The officer reached for the document. She pulled it away. "I'll hold," she said, "don't touch." He nodded, and walked away. *"Muchachos,"* he said to my brother and me, *"¿tienen papeles?"* Neither one of us said anything. I moved closer to my brother. He asked his question again. "I don't know what that is," I said. He smiled. "You're a U.S. citizen, are you?" "Yes, sir," we both said. "Who was the first president?" he asked. "That's easy," I said, "George Washington." He winked at us and kept walking down the row. I didn't go back to work until I knew my father was safe.

«1970»

The boy had grown up, looked almost like a man, but his eyes were still those of a child. These days were different for him: days of black armbands to protest the war that had lasted as long as the boy could remember; days of draft cards and draft numbers; days of putting up posters on his walls and making his father angry; days of examining his face in the mirror looking for signs of manhood; days of joining sit-down strikes to change the dress code at school. The boy was still listening to music, still in love with sound: Three Dog Night, Grand Funk Railroad, Crosby, Stills, Nash, and Young. In his spare time, the boy stared at the posters that surrounded him: Jimi Hendrix and Janis Joplin and Che Guevara. There were farm worker boycotts, but the boy did not think of the boycotts: he was in love with Joan Baez, dreamed of the barefoot madonna. He wanted to grow his hair long, but his father would not let him. He got angry but said nothing. Sometimes he was happy and angry at the same time, though he didn't know why. This was the year he was going to graduate. This was going to be *the* year, he told himself, the best year of his life.

Some nights he wrote to his brother who was in the war, and when he signed the letters he hated the whole world for taking his brother away.

His last semester in high school, the boy was confused, but he tried not to think about the chaos in his mind. Words swam up there like fish at the edge of a lake trying to flap themselves into the water, back into life. He tried not to think about the future since his father had already decided he would go to the local college, but he knew it wasn't just his father—it was money, no money, no money to go to a school far away. But the boy blamed his father. He tried to focus his attention on the enemy at hand: the high school. He fought his final days at school as if everything were a protest song—a stubborn song being banged out on a guitar.

He was getting good grades in everything except chemistry. If he didn't pass, he'd have to go to summer school because it was a required course. All those good grades, and it had come down to this. He was a borderline student in that class and he knew it, but there wasn't any time. There wasn't any time. And the teacher hated him. He could feel the teacher's hatred, the blue-eyed wrestling coach who favored athletes and nice-looking white girls. His brother wrote and told him to calm down, told him everything would be all right: "Just graduate and go to college. Do whatever it takes, just don't join the army."

His father had been sick, had been taken to the hospital where the doctors discovered he'd had a stroke. He was recovering at home, slowly, and the boy's mother signed up to work longer hours at the factory. The boy came home after school, made dinner for his younger brothers and his father. Afterwards, he went to work at a hamburger joint. He studied late at night, and he was too tired for chemistry. Sometimes, he would stay home from school and keep his father company, even though his father didn't say much. Talking didn't matter to his father—he just hated being alone. The boy wanted to speak, to say something, but there was little to talk about when he tried. He sometimes looked at his father's face, his graying moustache, and wondered if he would die, but then put the thoughts away like dirty clothes in a hamper. He thought instead of the chemistry teacher. He might have a better chance of passing the class if he took off the armband he wore every day to school, but his father was happy his son was wearing it. The boy and the father were together on the subject of the war.

The boy had missed too many days of school when his father had been unable to care for himself, but when he improved, the boy started getting back to his studies, back to his chemistry. "I have to pass this course," he told himself, "I have to. This can't keep me down. *This won't keep me down.*" He thought of all the work he'd done, all the *A*'s he'd made for his father, and now this—this because the old man had gotten sick. "He had to get sick," he mumbled. He clenched his jaw, did not say a word to anyone.

His father mentioned to him that the Brown Berets were coming to town. The boy laughed when his father told him his uncle had said they were just a bunch of punks. "Yeah," the boy answered, "Uncle Nacho also says that the peace sign is the footprint of the American chicken." They both laughed. The boy was happy when his father laughed.

"Chicano Power," the boy repeated to himself. The words sounded strange. The movement, the movement, it had come, had finally reached his hometown. It would change everything. Would it change everything? Anything? Anything at all? He read a poster calling for an all-out student strike, and music played in his head, music like he'd heard floating out of a forgotten hotel from his childhood. His father said they had the right idea but growled that they needed haircuts. The boy shook his head.

The Chicanos were going to strike. The boy wanted to be with them, wanted it, wanted to march. He was afraid, and he was angry with himself for being afraid. He kept studying. The students were asked to walk out of their classrooms, and the blue-eyed coach kept talking about what chemicals, when combined with others, caused an explosion. The boy smiled. He could hear the Chicanos coming down the hall: "…Chicano!" a voice yelled. "POWER!" the voices shouted back. Music, the boy thought, music. "Chicano … POWER … Chicano … POWER … Chicano … POWER …" The voices grew louder. The sound of marching feet echoed down the hall. They're dancing, the boy thought, and his feet shuffled under his desk. "Chicano…"

The wrestling coach stared at his class as the voices came closer. "No one is to leave this classroom—no one."

"…POWER!…"

"I don't like my class being interrupted. This is a school, not a playground for idiots." The boy listened to the sound of his teacher's voice. It sounded as if it were made of cardboard—nothing at all original in what he said, nothing interesting, just a voice, a voice addicted to the attention of his students.

"…POWER…"

The boy's friend looked at him, and words were written in his eyes: "The hell with him, come on…" The boy looked at his friend, and his eyes nodded. He wanted to dance, he wanted to sing, he wanted to answer: "The hell with him."

"If anyone leaves this classroom, I'm suspending them." The coach shut the door, his eyes bulged at his students. His eyes erased the color of most of his students. "We're all equal here—nobody's better than anybody else. They're just noise. This is the age of noise. No need for any of you to get involved. This is not the place…"

The boy's friend looked at him again.

The boy looked back, his brown eyes speaking: "I can't. He'll flunk me. Do you understand that I can't?"

"Chicano…" They were marching past the classroom. Hundreds of them. *Millions of us, millions.* The boy's heart shook. He thought it would shake forever.

"…POWER…"

His friend stared at him: "Now. Let's go. Now!"

I'll suspend anyone who leaves this class. The boy looked toward the door; he heard every footstep.

He looked at his friend and shook his head.

One of the marchers opened the door—raised a fist at the students sitting at their desks.

The boy's friend raised a fist, too. A salute; he held his fist high like a man reaching for something.

The wrestling coach glared at him.

The boy's friend glared back. He kept his fist up, then put it down—slowly. Deliberately. He smiled at the teacher.

The boy smiled, too. He didn't march. He passed the course. He graduated.

«*September 16, 1970*»

Dear Javier,

Well, I started college two weeks ago, and so far it seems to be OK. Nothing special. The old man's already on my case about studying, as if I was always messing around. I swear I don't understand that man. I don't think anyone does. And he never lets up.

School doesn't seem very hard, but I didn't think it would be. I guess you already know I didn't want to go to school here. I wanted to go to a better school—anywhere—just not here. I didn't want to live at home, but I guess I'll just have to deal with it. Anyway, Dad's happy about it. He's always talking about how he built those buildings and how they belong to us. Try telling that to the State!

I'm still working on weekends and even during the week sometimes. If I'm not working, I'm studying or going to class. I even find time to go to movies sometimes with our little brothers (who are now bigger than you and me). Somehow, they don't seem to ever change—they still think everything is funny. They have Mom's sense of humor. (Thank God!) And speaking of Mom, she's doing great. She looks a little tired sometimes, but she's alright. I think she worries about you a lot. She has your picture beneath the statue of the Virgin, and has a candle lit for you (of course!). The kids call it the eternal flame. Clowns! Mom says you look very handsome in a uniform. Personally, I think you look better in jeans.

Mom says Dad's taken to dreaming about you, but she says she can't get much out of him. I swear he gets more uncommunicative every day (if that's possible). He's so damn stubborn, and he's sick all the time. I think it's because he keeps everything in—it just eats at him. Anyway, enough of all that.

I don't have much time right now—I'm in between classes, but I at least wanted to drop you a note to let you know I think of you and miss you. It's strange. I sometimes think you'll come walking through the door any minute. Take care of yourself, OK? Watch out for Charlie. Write when you get a chance—your last letter was great (even though your penmanship sucks!).

Un abrazo,
Luis

«*1974*»

I graduated from college yesterday—from the university my father wanted me to attend. Somehow it was a letdown, but it was a letdown from the very beginning. This is not what I wanted. This is what my father wanted. I never said a word. He never lived to see me graduate.

Right after the ceremony I wanted to rush to the cemetery and throw my diploma on his grave and yell: "Goddamn you, there it is! There it is!" I couldn't quite bring myself to do it. Yelling at the dead seemed like such a stupid thing to do. I did go to the cemetery. I placed the diploma on my father's gravestone and said nothing. It was like he was still alive and I was simply giving him something he wanted, something he needed.

Looking at Dad's grave, I thought of the summer when he picked onions in the fields. For whatever reason, it was the only summer I remembered. I remembered him mocking the migrants when we came out of a barbershop one time—a vague memory, but I know it happened. And yet, when he was working in the fields, he seemed alive, a part of everything. Everyone liked him because he was so rebellious, and he made jokes about the gringos. Everyone would laugh. A man from that summer even went to my father's funeral. He told me my father was a good man. Yes, he was a good man, but that didn't make him any easier to love. I wish love had come as easy to him as work.

Standing there in the cemetery I suddenly remembered being afraid when the border patrol came looking for "wetbacks," and I couldn't go back to work until I knew my father was safe. Safe from what? I cut the weeds around the graves, and it made me think of the stems of the onions. I looked at the graves—my grandfather's, my father's, my brother's. "Remember, Javier, how I told you that we were all onions?" There was no answer. His voice was buried somewhere deep—in the land of the dumb. He was gone. They were all gone. I knew someday there would be a place for me next to them—in the company of men who did not speak.

«1985»

The young man in his early thirties drove into the parking lot of the grocery store. Lines were forming around his eyes, and his hair was prematurely graying. He checked his coat pocket for the list his wife had made for him that morning. The afternoon sun was so hot it seemed to be melting everything, but the man did not seem to be bothered by the heat. He had a sort of lazy walk, and he was singing to himself in Spanish, a song, a Mexican song that was always sticking in his mind, and he swayed his body to the internal rhythm.

Inside the grocery store, he grabbed a cart and pretended he was driving a car in a race. He laughed to himself. He had given up trying to change—now he just enjoyed the games he played. He looked over the list and headed for the fresh vegetables. He felt the heads of lettuce and talked to them. He found just the right one and tossed it in his basket as though it were a ball going through a hoop. He smiled. He picked out fresh cilantro, tomatoes, jalapeños. He tore a plastic bag from the roll hanging above the vegetables and waited behind two women who were standing above the onion bin.

"God," one of them said, "these onions are absolutely beautiful. What would we do without onions?"

"Eat boring food, I suppose," the other answered. "Who invented them anyway?"

The other lady laughed. "No one invented them—the farmers grow them. It's amazing how farmers can grow things, isn't it?"

"And the nice thing about onions is that they're so cheap."

The man with the moustache nodded to himself. For a moment he did not seem like the happy young man who had skipped into the grocery store. He looked like a lost child, fenced in, a little boy who was lost in the fields of a summer in a country he had left but still dreamed of—a country that had claimed him forever, a country he would never understand. "Onions *are* cheap," he said aloud, "dirt cheap."

A SILENT LOVE

The old man watched his ten-year-old grandson sleeping on the floor, his old, black eyes almost sticking to the boy's curled-up body. He studied the dark boy as he inhaled the comfortable air in the house that smelled of himself and his two grandsons. Too many years without women. Men, the air in the house smelled of men—years and years of men.

The boy's breathing reminded him of chants he only half-remembered from the days when his mother took him to pray in the monastery. He heard her voice in the boy's breathing: "We must pray for the sins of the world." He remembered that day when she was shot down by that man in the street, that man who was waving a gun in the air as if it were just a toy. "We must pray for the sins of the world."

"No, Mama," the old man said, "not for the sins of the world—the world gunned you down." He often spoke to her as he kept his eyes on his sleeping grandson, though he was only vaguely aware who he was speaking to. He stared at the boy breathing in and out: regular, musical, a whispering piano playing the same notes over and over and over. This was the closest he came to prayer anymore—watching his José sleep. He could almost see the boy's dreams. The boy had become his favorite book to read in the evenings. He memorized it.

His older grandson, Gregorio, walked in the front door, tired or sad or angry. He's too young to look like that, the old man thought. Soon, he will hate.

Gregorio looked at his grandfather and brother. They were as unmoving as the desert air in summer. Their lives did not seem to move. They were forever in this room as if they were waiting for something to happen, but they did not notice when something *did* happen. They seemed to Gregorio like objects in a still-life: softly painted in light and shadow, but not touchable. Something made them appear grotesque—disfigured. He did not want to be trapped in this scene, though he felt a certain comfort watching them from a distance. His grandfather looked up at him, and though his lips did not move, he seemed to smile. His grandfather often wore that almost hidden smile. Gregorio attributed that look to old age: it had permanently softened his grandfather's eyes, making him appear fragile and old and dying.

"He likes to sleep on the floor, doesn't he, Grandpo?"

The old man nodded.

"I wonder if he hears in his dreams?"

The old man shook his head.

"I wonder what all that silence is like?"

"Unimaginable, Greggy, an unimaginable silence. It gives him a kind of innocence, don't you think?"

"Oh, Grandpo, you always say things like that. Would you like to be deaf to preserve a look of innocence?" There was a touch of anger in his voice, a rough edge absent from his face when he wasn't speaking. It was as though his voice sandpapered his nearly perfect face like a rough beard.

"No," the old man answered, "No, I wouldn't—but that's only because I've gotten used to sound. Sound is what I know, but I'm not so sure anymore that most of the things I've heard were worth hearing. Who knows, maybe he's better off. I tell you, Greggy, my ears are rotting from the crap I've heard most of my life."

"Are you sure your ears aren't just rotting with age?" Gregorio grinned at his grandfather. He sat on the couch opposite him, his brother between them in the center of the room. He took off his shoes, leaned his head back, stared up at the ceiling, and yawned.

"Tired, Greggy?"

"Yeah, I guess. Long day."

"You don't have to work that job, Gregorio. It's not a great job. It takes you away from your studies."

"I like the job, Grandpo."

"What then, what? Why won't you take my money? Do you think I need it? Will you feel better about spending it after I'm dead?"

"Grandpo, you don't have that much money."

"I have enough. I have plenty."

"Let's not talk about this, Grandpo. I'm not quitting, OK?"

The old man shook his head and ran his rough hands through his thick, gray hair. "You're so—"

"So what?"

"So unhappy."

"No, I'm not."

"OK, you're happy. Sometimes you make me want to start smoking again."

"You have started again." Gregorio walked over to his grandfather's desk and opened the bottom drawer. He pulled out an open pack of cigarettes and an ashtray, placed them on the end table next to his grandfather's chair, and sat back down on the couch. He flashed his teeth at the old man and waited for him to defend his position.

"So, Mr. Detective, how long have you known?"

"Well, I don't think you've been at it very long. Those cigarettes weren't there two weeks ago."

"You go through my desk often, do you?"

"Grandpo, don't make me out to be a snoop. I was looking for some typing paper. It was an accident. It's not as if I were launching an investigation."

The old man laughed, reached for a cigarette, and lit it. "Good. I'm glad you found out. This way I won't have to go around hiding in my own house." He inhaled and blew out a giant smoke ring.

"How can you stand those things? And you were doing so well. You haven't touched one of those things in seven years. I was still a kid."

"Closer to nine years, Greggy—and you're still a kid. Back then, you used to enjoy my smoke rings."

"Twenty-one, Grandpo. Twenty-one isn't such a kid, and I'm not that impressed with smoke rings anymore."

"So you can drink in a bar and you can vote. Does that mean you're not a kid? And you don't even vote—"

"No lectures on voting, Grandpo, I'm not political."

The old man blew another smoke ring and kept himself from railing at his grandson. Not political, he mumbled to himself, not political.

"Your cigarette's polluting my air, Grandpo."

"Better watch it, Greggy, you're getting political."

"Very funny—don't change the subject."

"I'm not changing the subject. If you're interested in cleaning up the environment—a noble if political act—then I suggest you stop picking on the small fry and begin with some of those big corporations. I can provide you with a list if you like, Greggy. And you can also get rid of that car of yours—it's been polluting my air for the last couple of years."

Gregorio wanted to scream. "You're avoiding the issue."

"I am not avoiding the issue. What's the issue? The issue is that you hate smokers. Don't take the moral high ground and tell me the issue is clean air. As far as I can see, you don't give a damn about clean air. I'm an old man who has damn few pleasures. I smoke a few cigarettes a day— I'm not a chain-smoker, I'm not a criminal, and I'm tired of having no bad habits. And don't worry about the air in this house—you're not home enough to breathe any of it."

"What about José's air?"

The old man didn't answer. "So all of a sudden you're concerned about your brother?" he wanted to ask, but he swallowed the question. "If José doesn't like the air in this house, I'm sure he'll let me know—he's not one to hold things back. He's the biggest talker in this house."

Gregorio made himself smile. "You should have been a lawyer, Grandpo—you never lose an argument."

The old man laughed. "I've lost my share."

Greggy laughed. "When I have my own house, Grandpo, I'm not going to let you smoke in it."

"Yes, you will. I'll walk into your house, hug your kids, have a beer with you, and light up. I bet you won't throw me out either."

"You don't play fair, old man."

"You remind me of your grandmother, Gregorio. There was something very tough about her exterior and something soft underneath."

"I don't have anything soft underneath, Grandpo."

The old man nodded. "Have it your way, Greggy." He finished his cigarette and smiled, his yellow teeth white in the dimly lit room. "It's time for me to take your brother to his bed." He rose slowly from his chair, bent down, and picked up the boy—softly—with knowing hands. Sure movements. He breathed heavily as he balanced the boy in his arms. The boy did not wake, but his hands reached up around the old man's neck.

"Why don't you just wake him, Grandpo? He's not a baby anymore. He can walk to his room. He's deaf, not lame."

"What you also mean is that I'm getting too old to carry him into his bedroom."

"That, too, Grandpo. Remember, you're fifty-two years older than me."

The old man shook his head and pressed the boy close to him. He walked quietly down the hall and placed the boy in his bed. He carefully took off his clothes and covered him in blankets. He watched him, combed his hair with his hands, and kissed him. He lingered for a moment, and then moved toward the door, leaving his smell in the room.

Gregorio waited in the living room. He held on to the image of his grandfather carrying his brother. They seemed like dancers. He turned their image over in his mind, noticing how small his brother looked, an object that would break if dropped. His grandfather's steps were sure. He seemed so large when he stood—even now in his seventies. He thought of the odd relationship between Grandpo and José. Sometimes they were playmates playing marbles or checkers. Sometimes they were best friends—equals—as if they had worked together at the same factory for years. Sometimes, it was José who seemed older, taking care of the old man. And there was always so much touch between them, as if touching had replaced speaking. They seemed not to need or expect anything from the outside world—seemed untouched by the confusions and preoccupations of existence. Even now, when they walked together, José took his grandfather's hand when other ten-year-old boys had outgrown such little boy ways. He did not understand their love. He felt left out, yet he knew it was a strange feeling, since he did not really *want* to be included.

The old man walked back into the living room. He stepped into the kitchen and came back with two beers. He handed one to Gregorio.

"You spoil him too much, Grandpo." He twisted off the cap to his beer.

The old man concentrated on the taste of the beer and did not seem to hear the sound of Gregorio's voice. "Good beer," he said. "Yes, I spoil him. I'd spoil you, too, if you'd let me."

"I don't need to be carried to my bedroom."

"That's not what I meant."

Gregorio sipped his beer and did not respond to his grandfather's remark. They drank in silence. They could hear the passing cars outside the house.

"I don't know how else to love him, Greggy." And I don't know how to love you either, he said to himself. "And you should spend more time with him. All you have to do is try—talk. Just talk to him. He reads lips, and you know sign language. Talk to him."

"It's hard sometimes."

"He's not hard to please—all you have to do is ask him something."

"Like what?"

"Is affection for a brother so hard?"

Gregorio looked up at the ceiling. "Yes—it's hard."

The old man lit a cigarette, took a puff, put it out. He rose stiffly from his chair and locked his jaw. "I'll finish my beer over a book in my room." He spoke with his back to his grandson.

"Don't stay up too late, Grandpo," he said quietly.

The old man did not respond as he walked down the hall.

César opened the book and began reading at the place where he had left off. The place was marked with a holy card he had kept from his wife's funeral, a holy card as worn as his hands. After reading more than a page he realized he did not remember what he had read. "Ahhh," he said, "words, words, words." His anger at Gregorio caught in his throat. "I don't like the way he's turning out, Adela." He sneered at himself for speaking to his wife who had been dead for twenty years. "I don't know what's happening to him, Adelita. *Tu sabes como son los hijos.* Maybe there just weren't enough women around. I just didn't have the energy to remarry." He stopped talking and sipped on his beer. "I'm just a god-damned fool talking to the dead—a sure sign I'll be joining them soon." He finished his beer slowly and turned off the light. He lay in his bed and thought about the things he should say to Gregorio: "Look, Greggy, you don't let anybody into that world of yours. You're going to get awful lonely… Look, Greggy, I know it was hard for you when your mother died—it was hard for all of us, but my God, you're getting hard… No, Greggy, I don't love your brother more—don't be stupid. And stop feeling guilty about him. It's nobody's fault he's deaf. Come on, Greggy, stop it…" *Tomorrow, I'll talk to him.*

Gregorio sat at his desk making a list of things that had to be done in the morning:

        —finish reading Chapter Ten
        —study session with Gary (4th floor of library, 1:30)
        —balance check book / make deposit
        —buy flowers for Rachel

He crossed out the last item on the list, put the piece of paper in his backpack, cleared off his desk, and kicked off his tennis shoes without untying them. He fell into bed with his journal in his hand and opened it to the first empty page. He could think of nothing to write. Rachel's going to leave. He wanted to write the thought down, but he didn't want to see the words, didn't want to read them to himself. He thumbed through the journal, re-reading the fragmented writing. He ran across an entry he had written one night after a storm, a storm that had jarred him from sleep:

> It was all so silent. The rain stopped. And then the wind died—sudden—outside, it was silent. I could hear nothing in all the deadness, and my own breathing, like the night, was soundless. I wanted the morning to come, wanted to hear a bird shatter the quiet. But it was too early for the birds to be singing. I lay still in my bed that held no lovers—a bed that, if it could talk, would have nothing to say.

He was embarrassed by his own writing. He threw the journal on the floor, turned off the light, and took off his clothes in the dark.

César woke in the morning remembering his dream. The dream was familiar now—this was the fourth time it had come to him in a year. In the dream he was sleeping and something woke him. His eyes opened and all the lights in the house were on. Outside it was still night. This did not scare him. Inexplicably, he got up to put an album on his record player, the record player that had once belonged to his wife. When the music began, he started to sing. It was then he realized no sound was coming out of his mouth. He came to the sudden realization that he had lost his voice—forever. He began to cry. He turned off the lights, but the room remained lit. He found himself painting furiously—painting a huge canvas. While he was painting, the room grew black and dark. He turned on the light to see what he had painted, and he found a book instead of a painting—a black book with his name written on the cover.

César recalled his dream and turned it over in his mind. He had concluded that the dream was about death. He was not disturbed, was not afraid, was not even uneasy. It made him feel peaceful—like standing on a beach facing an ocean that was at once violent and quiet.

He remembered a conversation he once had with José, who had asked him if he were afraid to die, but he had signed it in an odd way. He had asked José to write down the question, and he had written on the pad: "Are you afraid of touching the infinite?" He had thought it a strange expression for a ten-year-old boy to use, but he had ceased being surprised by his grandson's sensitivity and facility with words. "Do you mean, am I afraid of dying?" José had nodded. "No," César had told him, "no, I'm not afraid. I'll see your grandmother and your mother, too." José smiled. It was the truth—half the truth, anyway. César did not believe there was such a thing as the "whole truth"—nothing was whole. He didn't believe in heaven or hell, had stopped believing with the death of his mother. The death of his wife and his daughter only confirmed that there was no sensible force that moved the universe. He believed only in the goodness and the cruelty of human beings. It was enough for him to handle—more than enough.

He thought of José's phrase: touching the infinite. He believed in that, but it was not quite the same thing that José had in mind. I've touched the infinite, he thought. The image of a girl appeared before him, a girl he knew briefly when he was young. They had not made love, but she had looked at him once in a way that made him feel naked. He had felt that she knew everything about him; he was not ashamed, was not afraid. She had stared, saturated his skin with her eyes, anointed him with her look. Miraculously he was clean—only for an instant—but he was clean. And he remembered his wife telling him she was pregnant. She had taken his hand and opened it as wide as she could—stretching it. She touched every line lightly with her fingers. "I love your hands, César." He still remembered the sound of her voice, her lips, her young face that did not speak of hope—but was hope itself. Yes, that was touching the infinite. He remembered holding his daughter before she died—that look of want and hurt and expectation that her illness would be no more. Yes, that was touching the infinite. He felt he'd touched it three times already—so what was death? He shook his head in mild disgust. He hurried from his bed realizing that if José was not yet awake he would be late to school.

José smiled at his grandfather as he walked into the kitchen. The old man touched his grandson's head lightly and moved toward the coffee pot. "Good coffee," the old man signed, "nice and strong." José winked at his grandfather and laughed. He noticed the old man's hands. He felt sad for a moment knowing his Grandpo was growing old. He did not remember his mother, but he had a picture of her, and he knew that people died and he was afraid sometimes. But when his grandfather signed words to him, the boy felt that the old man's hands moved like wings. He can almost fly, José thought.

He watched his grandfather read the newspaper, his lips moving slightly as he read. Sometimes the old man would shake his head and José wondered what he was thinking. José looked at his watch, saw that it was almost time, and tapped his grandfather's newspaper. The old man looked up: "Is it time to go?" José nodded. They walked outside together and waited for the school van in the front yard. José held his books and leaned against his grandfather. After a few minutes he saw the van from his school turn the corner. He looked up at his Grandpo, kissed him on the cheek, and waved good-bye. "Learn," his grandfather signed to him, "learn."

Gregorio woke from his sleep and tried to push away the dream he'd been having. He knew his mother was in the dream and that she'd spoken to him. He hated having them, hated remembering them. But he was not a believer in dreams. He cleared his mind and thought of other things. He imagined that Rachel was lying next to him. He fought the urge to masturbate and forced himself to get out of bed. In the shower, he imagined Rachel was with him.

César walked back into the kitchen and poured himself a second cup of coffee. Gregorio walked into the room and filled a glass with orange juice. "Anything in the newspaper?"

"The world's at war," the old man answered.

"Anywhere in particular?" Gregorio smiled slightly.

"Just pick a spot."

Gregorio poured himself a cup of coffee. "José gone?"

The old man nodded. "He's in a play next week. I want you to go. He'd like you to go."

"When next week?"

"Wednesday."

"I work Wednesday nights, Grandpo."

The old man folded his newspaper. "Get the night off. Can't you trade nights with someone?"

Gregorio hesitated. "Well, maybe. I'll have to see."

César was quiet for a moment. "Your brother's in a play. Get the night off." The command sounded strange—his voice had been harsher than he had intended.

Gregorio looked at his grandfather, but showed no expression. "I said I'd have to see. I can't just take off from work anytime I want."

"Last week you traded a night to go to a concert. If you can do that, then you can go to your brother's play."

"A deaf play?"

The old man bit his lip and pulled at his collar. He took a slow, unsteady drink from his coffee. "Yes, a deaf play. What is it with you, Greggy?"

"Why are you always on my case about José?"

"You never see him."

"It can't be helped."

"The hell it can't."

"Look, I'm working, and I'm going to school. It's hard, Grandpo. It won't be this way forever—just for a while."

"It will always be this way with you, Greggy. It has always been this way. Do you know you've never done anything with your brother, not even when he was a little boy? You've never even tossed a football with him."

"He never liked football."

The old man shook his head. "You're a stranger in this house. 'He never liked football'—that's what you have to say? A stranger to your own brother. What happens between the two of you when I'm dead?"

"Why are you always talking about death? Stop talking about that! You're still healthy."

"For how long, Greggy? I have dreams."

"Dreams? You have dreams?"

"Yes, I have dreams."

"I have dreams, too—and I want a life."

"Ahh, you want to be free, is that it? That doesn't make you very different from your brother—or me. We all want to be free of things. We're not birds, Greggy—we don't goddamn fly."

"Who said anything about flying? I just want to finish school. Things will settle down for me, Grandpo. You'll see."

"Gregorio, nothing's going to change until you do something about your attitude toward your brother."

"What attitude is that?"

"Why do you resent him?"

"I do not resent him."

"The hell you don't. You act as if you might catch his deafness. It's not a communicable disease."

"Will you lay off?"

"No, I won't lay off. We have to talk about this, Greggy—"

"I'm already late." Gregorio stood up and started for the door.

"Sit down, Greggy."

"You're acting like an old woman."

The old man could not hide his surprise at the words. He ground his teeth and slammed an open palm on the table.

"It's true, Grandpo, you've turned into an old woman. You don't do anything but grow flowers and cook. Ever since Mom died you started acting like a woman. I hate it. I really hate it."

The old man fought the urge to slap his grandson. He felt his face turning red; he placed his hands together and popped his knuckles.

Gregorio opened his mouth and continued, "Men don't—"

César stuck his hand out and stopped him. "That's enough, Gregorio. I've heard enough." He pushed his gray hair back with his fingers. "You don't like what I've become, eh? Well, I don't like what you've become either. You're a cold young man. You're embarrassed by feelings. Isn't that sad, Greggy? Isn't that sad? Someday you'll rot in all that silence—"

"Gra—"

The old man raised his hand again and stopped Gregorio from speaking. "I don't want to hear it, Greggy. You're not a child anymore. Maybe you never were—maybe you stopped being a boy when your mother died. Well, what's to be done? What could any of us have done?" His voice quieted into a whisper, as if something inside was wearing down, wearing out. "She died, your mother—and your brother's deaf, but you can't accept that, can you? You fight everything around you. You even fight affection. I've tried not to fight back. Maybe I was wrong. But other people, Greggy, other people will fight back—and they won't give a damn. A woman," he repeated, "an old woman. An old woman? Because I love my children? I'm sick about this, Greggy." The old man rose slowly from his chair. He walked toward the door leading to the garden.

Gregorio drove to work without noticing he was at the wheel. He thought about Rachel, her soft brown eyes asking him questions. He was pushing her away, didn't know how to pull her close. He knew she would leave. She had mentioned she needed to talk to him, but he had avoided her for the last few days, afraid of what she might say. Maybe he wouldn't have to listen. Maybe he'd just never call her again and they could just forget about it. He tried to push her away from his thoughts. He clutched the wheel of the car and turned on the radio, but the music was distant. He heard his grandfather's voice: "Someday you'll rot—" He watched himself standing over his grandfather and yelling: "A woman, an old woman." He wanted to shake himself, be someone else, something else, anything else. "Grandpo, it's all wrong—I don't know how to talk…" He reached the library, almost running over a student crossing the street. He sat in the car and rested his head on the steering wheel.

César lit a cigarette in the back yard and stood in the late morning light. He'd spent the morning pulling weeds. "That's what I do," he said out loud, "I pull weeds. They grow back. I pull them. And goddamn it if they won't outlive my flowers." He wondered what his wife and daughter would think about his garden. They'd like it, he thought, they'd put the flowers in vases all over the house.

José looked out the window and saw his brother's car coming up the driveway. His brother looked tired, looked as though his head were too heavy for his body. A small blue car drove up and parked in front of the house. His brother's girlfriend, whom he'd met only once, got out of the car. He saw them talking. He could see their faces, their moving lips, but he could not understand the words they were uttering. He knew they were angry by the way they were standing, by the way they were moving their arms. He knew they must be yelling. They talked for what seemed like a long time. He watched his brother's face get angrier and angrier, until all José saw was a grimace covering his entire face. It was the most emotion he'd ever seen his brother wear.

He saw his brother's girlfriend shaking her head in response to a question. She took off a small chain she wore around her neck and placed it in Gregorio's hands. He dropped it on the ground. She turned from him and walked toward the car. José could see she was crying. She got in her car and drove away. He watched his brother stare at the empty space where her car had been. He could see that he was saying something to himself. His lips were moving, and José thought his face would burst in anger. Gregorio did not move for a long time. José stood breathless—watching his brother. The old man sat in the dining room watching his grandson staring out the window.

At dinner, no one spoke. César had not acknowledged Gregorio's presence when he came in the house. Gregorio mumbled something about the food being good. "Like women's cooking?" César asked. Gregorio did not answer. José understood the words his grandfather had spoken, but he did not understand what the words meant. He knew his grandfather and his brother were angry; they often acted this way after a fight. He kept his eyes on the food, occasionally looking up at both of them. It had never been this bad. He wanted to ask them why they were mad, but he knew they wouldn't tell him, so he ate his dinner and tried to keep his hands still. He watched his brother's hands as he ate. They were shaking.

After dinner, Gregorio washed the dishes. José sat at the kitchen table, wanting to talk to him. Gregorio did not notice him, and after he finished cleaning up, he walked to his room. He tried to study, tried not to think of Rachel or his grandfather or his brother. He could not concentrate on his homework. He kept staring at the pages, thinking he'd just quit school, quit his job, quit everything. The hell with it all, he thought. Maybe I'll just move out.

José walked into his bedroom. "Hi," he waved. Gregorio was surprised at his brother's visit. He never came into his room. José sat on the bed and bounced on it. "Are you studying?" he signed.

Gregorio nodded.

"Do you like it?"

"No," Gregorio signed back, "I hate it."

"I hate math, too. I'm not good at things like that."

Gregorio smiled. They sat quietly for a moment and said nothing.

"Well," José signed after a few minutes of silence. "I better let you study. I have to finish my homework, too." He jumped off the bed and touched his brother on the shoulder. "Will you come to my play?"

Gregorio smiled awkwardly and nodded.

José walked toward the door, but turned as his hand touched the doorknob. He looked at his older brother. "Does it hurt?" he signed.

"Does what hurt?"

José wanted to point to his heart, but his hands froze. He waited for a moment. He wanted to tell Gregorio that he had seen him fighting with his girlfriend, tell him that he knew he was sad, but he was afraid Gregorio would get angry. He looked at his brother and was unable to move his hands. He shrugged his shoulders and left the room.

Gregorio walked out of his room after studying for the evening. He stood in the doorway of the living room and watched his grandfather watching José asleep on the floor. "Nothing ever changes around here, does it?"

The old man looked up. "No, I guess not."

"Would you like a beer, Grandpo?"

The old man nodded. Gregorio walked into the kitchen and brought in two beers. He handed one of them to his grandfather. "Let me put your brother to bed." The old man rose from the chair and picked José up, re-enacting the nightly balancing act, the nightly waltz. Gregorio watched his grandfather's skilled movements. The old man stood still for a moment holding his grandson in his arms. Gregorio wanted them to stay in front of his eyes forever. "Grandpo," he said, "don't ever die."

"It's a promise I can't make, Greggy," he said.

Gregorio swallowed, fought to hold back tears that were stronger than his will. The old man stared at him and smiled. Reluctantly he disappeared down the hall with José in his arms. Gregorio walked toward his grandfather's desk and pulled out the ashtray and cigarettes. He placed them on the end table next to the old man's chair. He sat in the center of the room where his brother had been sleeping. It was warm there. He waited for his grandfather to step back into the room.

FLOWERS FOR THE BROKEN

«I»

Her skin is the color of a brown paper bag; her eyes are a dull cactus color, drought green. She dresses like a man: men's jeans, men's shoes and socks, and oversized long-sleeved shirts. She hides her body, not because her body is ugly but because she does not like to think about it. And she does not like others to think about it either.

She looks like a child as she sleeps, though she is a woman in her early twenties. She lies in a bed that has known no one but her, and she is dreaming. She does not like dreams; she does not like what they remind her of; she does not admit they exist. She dreams anyway, but it does not matter since she has no memory of them.

"It's time to get up," she hears her mother say, a voice like an alarm clock. She feels her mother tap her on the shoulder and shake her awake: "Come on, Angel, you'll be late. Come have your coffee, it's waiting." She listens to her mother's footsteps as she paces into the kitchen. Opening her eyes, she shuts them again, does not want this day to begin. She hugs herself for an instant, just long enough to feel her skin tingle, then pulls her hands away in disgust. She does not like the feeling of her own skin. She lies still for a moment and thinks about the coming day. How many flower deliveries? How many door bells to ring? How many dull expressions of gratitude? She imagines the voices of the women who arrange flowers, hears their unceasing complaints: *No one sends me these, no one ever does.* She sees their working hands de-thorning roses. She sees handwriting on cards she isn't supposed to read. She laughs to herself at the things people write on those cards attached to the flowers. *Do they mean what they say, do they mean it? Do they ever hear themselves?*

She places her feet on the floor; it does not feel real or solid. Cotton.

For a minute she thinks the floor will not hold her up, but then she discovers she can walk. A miracle, she thinks, like walking on water or on summer clouds that she used to watch as a little girl. She puts on her bathrobe and walks into the kitchen. The sun floods into the room and shines on her face, and for a second she looks like her name. Her mother places a cup of coffee in front of her. "Did you sleep well, sweetheart?"

She nods. "Like an angel." Her mother laughs, but Angel does not smile at her own joke. She hates her nickname. She wishes her mother would call her Angelica. Angel sounds to her as if she should be walking around wearing a first communion dress. *I'm too old to be called Angel*, she wants to say, *I don't want to be your angel.*

"I dreamed of your father last night," her mother says. "Do you know, I like dreaming of him now that he's gone." She smiles at her daughter. "Do you ever dream of him?"

Angel shakes her head.

"You used to dream of him all the time—but you were a little girl. Little girls dream about everything." She pulls up a chair across from her daughter and opens the newspaper. Angel knows she will turn to the obituary page and say: *Fulana de Tal died. Poor thing. Dios la tenga en paz.* She waits for her mother to find the news of death and to announce the news so she can nod.

"Well, Doña Estefanita finally died," her mother says, lifting her head above the newspaper. "It was her time. She was ninety-two. Too old. God, I don't want to live to be that old. Please, God, take me sooner than that. She was a good woman, Estefanita—do you remember her?"

Angel nods, though she does not remember Estefanita. She remembers none of her mother's friends. They were all the same to her—even smelled the same.

"*Dios la tenga en paz.* She had a miserable husband. God, forgive him. He made a pass at me once when I was a young woman. He was old enough to be my father, but he didn't care. He tried to fool around with every woman he met. Some women liked him, I suppose, and Doña Estefanita never said a word about his unfaithfulness. She just took it all in silence. And he wasn't even good-looking. He was her cross, but now she'll have some rest."

Angel repeats the last words to herself: "Now she'll have some rest." Her mother says something like this every morning. When there is no news of someone's death, she makes the sign of the cross and says:

"Tomorrow there will be two." There is something both repugnant and comforting in her mother's predictability. Angel sips on her coffee, swishing the bitterness around in her mouth. She knows her mother will now turn to the vital statistics to see who has gotten a license to get married or to find out who has had a baby. It is always the same. Angel seems to follow her mother's every word, but she is only half-listening. She has trained herself to look interested when her mother speaks.

"Teresa and Tomás are getting a divorce," she announces. "They've only been married two years. I suppose Teresa will go back to live with her mother. She'll need help raising her little boy—and their house is so small. Already they're too crowded in that small house of theirs. You know, Teresa's father never provided them with a good house. Don't ever get married, Angel." She looks at her daughter.

"No, Mama, I never want to get married." Angel looks up in the air as if she is looking at the words she has just spoken. She wants to look at the words to see if she believes them.

Her mother smiles. "Men are a lot of trouble. Your father was— well, never mind about that. Men are at their best when they are in your dreams, and that is the only place where they belong."

Angel nods. She thinks her neck is going to break from all the nodding she does. She smiles at her own thought, and her mother thinks she is smiling at her. She tries to imagine her mother as a young woman. She must have been very beautiful. But she is harsh; her smile is shiny and hard like unbreakable glass. *Smiles are for the young,* her mother once told her, *or for the very old.* Angel watches her mother light a cigarette and turn the pages of the newspaper. Her mother smokes three cigarettes a day: one in the morning, one in the evening, and one before she goes to bed. Angel wishes she would quit, or better, she wishes she would lose control and smoke all day long. *Even this she will control, even her cigarettes.* "I'll have to call Estefanita's daughter," her mother says, half to Angel and half to herself.

Angel watches her mother for a moment longer. She whispers her mother's name to herself: Rosa. She does not know why she whispers it. She gets up slowly and walks to the bathroom. She takes off her robe and looks at her body in the mirror. Her body is perfect, but she does not see it. She shakes her head and tries to push her breasts in. The hot water and the soap against her skin feel good—showers are the only times she ever feels happy to have a body. She imagines that the water falling down on her is rain. Maybe, she thinks, something will grow inside me. She listens to herself whispering and tries to recognize her own voice. She steps out of the shower and dries herself. She dresses quickly and braids her hair while it is still wet. She has the urge to cut off her braid, but her mother would never forgive her. She does not look in the mirror to see what she looks like as she walks back out into the kitchen.

«*II*»

Angel's mother dropped her off in front of the flower shop. "Drive carefully today," her mother warned her. "You know how the people of this city drive—like a bunch of idiots. They don't know what signal lights are for. They're all ignorant—most of them from Juárez. Just keep a hand on the horn and pray." Angel smiled, nodded, and squeezed her mother's hand. She waved good-bye. She wondered why her mother always said such ugly things about the people of El Paso who came from Juárez, because her mother had been raised in Mexico, too. "Poor Mom," she said out loud, "all she ever does is complain—complain and worry. She thinks I'm still a girl. I'm not one of your belongings, Mama—be twenty-three next month." But her mother had driven away, did not hear her.

Angel stared at the sign in front of the flower shop. The name was written in big red letters: PAINT THE WORLD WITH ROSES. Angel shook her head at the sign. "What a stupid name for a flower shop," she muttered to herself. She was embarrassed by it. Mrs. Ayala, the boss's wife, had told her with such pride that when the flower shop first opened, they had held a contest to come up with a name for the flower shop. *And I chose the winning submission,* she had said, *Isn't it wonderful? Isn't it?* Angel had smiled at her in the same way she smiled at her mother. The motto had been added on the boss's fortieth birthday—a public gift from his wife: "Let a flower be your umbrella." Angel thought it was grounds for divorce. Every day she read those words. Every day, she wanted to hit the woman who had chosen that stupid and tasteless name for a flower shop—and a motto that made a Hallmark card appear cynical. "I'd like to take that sign and break it over her head," she said to herself. She pictured it, then laughed. She could see the letters of the sign smashing into the woman's skull—back into the place where they came from.

She walked into the shop and waved at the flower arrangers who already had deliveries ready for her. She heard Irma, the head flower arranger, complain about the boss's wife: "That woman and her god-damned coats. I'd like to strangle her with those necklaces she wears, necklaces her husband buys her with the money he makes off the skill of my hands." Angel heard her complaints and nodded—but she said noth-ing. Irma was right, she thought, but she did not feel anything for her. She did not feel a part of these women's lives—they would never be friends; they would never even be allies. They're too much like my moth-er, she thought, they don't like men—but they don't like women either.

She looked at the bouquets ready for delivery. She placed each bou-quet carefully in the truck and made a list of all the addresses. She took out her map and found one of the streets that she could not place. *I'll have to remember that street.* She didn't like not knowing where a street was. She wanted to know every street, memorize it. If she knew every vein of the city, then she was closer to knowing its heart, though she didn't know why she felt this.

She took a good look at all the flowers to see if any of them might carry a card with an interesting message. The big white box with two dozen roses would carry a message worth reading. *Yes, that one might be good.* She hated herself for reading the cards that went with the flowers, but something made her hand reach for the envelopes and open them— not all of them. *I shouldn't be doing this. Why do I do this?* But what dif-ference did it make? What did it matter? It didn't hurt her—and it didn't hurt anybody else either. Who did she talk to besides her mother? She would never tell anyone about the things she read, never reveal their con-fessions. And no one said anything original anyway. They all said un-believably stupid things. And they always signed their cards, "With love." From the looks of the cards she read, there was a lot of love in the world, but it didn't seem to Angel that El Paso was dying from too much love. *Shit, half the people here are starving to death—from all that love, I suppose.*

She loaded up the truck with the day's first deliveries and headed for the first address. She had several deliveries to offices downtown. She noticed that the box with two dozen roses was to be delivered to Sharon Gutierrez on the tenth floor of the State National Bank. In front of the bank, she parked the truck, and then read the card: "Sharon, last night was heaven. Really! Here's to more heavens." There was no signature, but Angel figured no signature was needed. She placed the note carefully back where it belonged and smiled to herself. People were so dumb, she thought. They never said anything amusing or remotely intelligent. It didn't much matter if the cards attached to the flowers were from men or from women—they were all dull and predictable. They had something in common with her mother. *More heavens! Get off it. And in a month, Sharon, where will you be? He'll be writing another dopey note to another dopey woman—and I'll be delivering the flowers.* She made a face. Reaching the tenth floor she asked a man where she might find Sharon Gutierrez. He directed her to a desk where a woman was typing a letter. She was dressed in a tight black sweater and two huge earrings dangled from her ears. Her face was dark and soft and she wore very little make-up. She was pretty in a very plain sort of way. Her hair was long and black and her nails were painted bright pink.

"Sharon Gutierrez?" Angel asked. "These are for you."

Sharon took the box and reached for the note. "Oh," she said, "Oh, thank you, thank you!" Angel thought she sounded like a high-school girl—one of the high-school girls chased by all the boys—high-school girls she had hated.

"Don't thank me," Angel smiled, "I just deliver them."

"But doesn't it make you feel good to know that you bring other people happiness?"

"I don't bring other people happiness," Angel said seriously, "I just deliver flowers."

Sharon smiled at her. "Same thing. Doesn't it feel good to have such a wonderful job?"

"It would feel better if I got paid more."

Sharon laughed. She opened the note and read it. "Oh, oh, oh," she whispered, "God bless that man." Angel stared at her. She wanted to ask her if it really was heaven. It couldn't have been that good. She kept looking at Sharon, who was deeply absorbed in staring at her roses and thinking of last night. She wondered what she would look like in Sharon's clothes. She shook her head and started to walk away.

"Thanks for delivering these," Sharon said, "you're an absolute angel."

"Yes, I know." Maybe, Angel thought, she would start wearing her hair differently. Maybe she would untie her long braid and let everybody see that she had the most beautiful hair in all of El Paso, beautiful, beautiful, beautiful. "But no one would notice," she said to herself. She reached the door to the elevator and pushed the button to go down.

Angel made the rest of the flower deliveries without thinking very much about the cards and the messages they contained. Most of the deliveries were daisies and carnations, nothing that caught her drought-green eyes. Most of the bouquets were for older ladies, so she guessed the flowers were being sent by children or grandchildren who couldn't—or wouldn't—make a visit. When she handed one of the bouquets of carnations to an old lady, all she said was: "*Ya nadie me visita*. They send me flowers, but they never even bother to call me. I open the cards to their flowers and they say they love me. Ha!"

She took a look at one of the cards attached to some white daisies. "Grandma, I love you so much. May the blessed Virgin keep you always. Happy Birthday. Your loving granddaughter, Ysela." She thought of her mother, who said virginity was the highest state a woman could reach. *Don't ever get married.* Angel shook her head. She disapproved of her mother's theology. She did not think of virginity very much; she didn't think about sex either. She looked in the rear view mirror and wondered what she would look like with make-up on. She touched herself, and then pulled her hand away. "I hate flowers," she whispered, "I hate them." She had the urge to rip up the white daisies with her indelicate hands and throw them on the street. She picked them up, stared at them for a moment, and quickly left them at the door without waiting to see if anyone was home. She hoped someone would steal them.

The last delivery of the morning was a basket of fruit with one red rose sticking out from the clear cellophane. She drove to an office building and parked the truck. She opened the card: "Michael, forgive me, but I can't go back to you. I just can't. Please understand. Carmen." She wondered what Carmen looked like; she wondered why Carmen bothered to send anything at all. If it was over, then what was the point? "She shouldn't tease him like this," she said to herself, "he'll just feel worse. Poor Carmen. Poor Michael." She wondered what they had been through together. Maybe they were both married. She took the basket to an office and asked for Michael McMullen. The secretary pointed to his office and smiled as she noticed the basket with the rose. Angel knocked at the door and waited until a voice asked her to come in.

Angel pushed the door open. "For you," she said.

"Who from?" he asked.

"Don't know. I just deliver."

He reached for the card but did not open it. He stared at it and ran his fingers on the edges of the small envelope. He seemed afraid to open it. He looked up and smiled, but he could not hide the sadness. "Do I owe you anything?" he asked.

"They're paid for," she said.

"Are you allowed a tip?"

"Yeah, sure."

He stood up, reached into his pocket, and gave her a five-dollar bill. His hand met Angel's for a second. "Thank you," he said.

She looked into his calm black eyes. "I'm just doing my job," she smiled. He was handsome, she thought. Kind, his eyes were kind. Maybe Carmen was an idiot. His voice was as soft as his eyes. She wanted to touch him. She turned around and walked out the door, placing the five dollars in her pocket.

She drove the truck back to the flower shop to pick up more flowers. The boss was in. "How's the truck?" he asked. "Is she giving you any trouble?"

It's not a she, she thought, it's a he. "No, sir, she's driving just fine."

"Why does everybody call that thing a truck?" Irma asked as she walked in from the back room. "It's not a truck, it's a van."

"Well, we like to call it a truck, don't we, Angel?" He winked at her.

"Yeah, sure." She didn't like it when he winked at her.

Irma shook her head. "The world's a goddamned mess. Call it a truck if you want. Call it any damn thing you want—call it a tractor, but just don't complain if I start calling the roses carnations or if I start calling funeral wreaths rainbows. Confusion is par for the course around this dump. If a thing has a name, call it by its right name. How the hell can we communicate if we just call everything any damn thing we want?"

"Irma, I never know what you're saying anyway." The boss laughed.

"Especially when I ask for a raise." She glared at him, and then looked over at Angel. "Angel, you got those twelve orders to deliver. After that it's quits for the day. Tomorrow, be here early because we're going to have you on the road all day. Two funerals, and lots of birthdays. We've also got a lot of flower deliveries to the hospitals—more babies. There's entirely too much screwing going on around this town. You may have to put in a few extra hours of overtime, so see to it that you get paid for it." She glanced at Mr. Ayala and walked into the back room.

"Don't you love how they love me." He smiled. He reminded Angel of Michael. "Someday I'm going to fire that woman."

"Why don't you do it now?" Angel asked.

"Because I like her."

"She doesn't seem to like you very much, does she?"

"Oh, she likes me fine—it's just her way. She gets mad at me because she hates my wife."

Angel said nothing. She wanted to end the conversation. Mr. Ayala was easy to talk to, but she didn't trust him. She didn't like people who talked so easily. She picked up a bouquet of flowers and started toward the truck. Mr. Ayala picked up a large bouquet and followed her. "You don't like my wife either, do you?"

"That's not true," Angel said. "I don't think about it."

"What do you think about?"

She went inside for more flowers.

He followed her. "Don't you ever talk to anybody about anything, Angel?"

"When I feel like talking, I say it with flowers."

Mr. Ayala laughed. They placed the last of the flowers carefully in the back of the truck. "When you finish today," he told her, "take the truck home. Like Irma said, you need to be here early tomorrow. No need for your mom to drive downtown just to bring you to work so early in the morning. We have a lot of deliveries. Tomorrow two funerals, and Saturday, four weddings. Love and death are great for business." He laughed at his own joke.

"Yeah, sure. We can cover just about anything with flowers, can't we?" Mr. Ayala patted her on the back. She stiffened and jerked slightly. She opened the door to the driver's seat. "Angel?" he said.

"Yes, sir?"

"How come you never dress up?"

"I don't work in an office, sir," she said. "I drive around town and deliver flowers. Should I dress up for that?"

"Well, it's not that you have to dress up a certain way to make deliveries, but you could dress up if you wanted to. I mean you might even attract some men. You're a nice-looking young woman, you know that, don't you?"

"Yes, I know that," she said. She hated him for saying it. What she looked like wasn't any of his business. She couldn't help but frown.

"Why are you frowning?"

"If I were a man, would you care what I dressed like?"

"Look, Angel, I'm not putting the moves on you. Don't get so defensive. I like you. But I'm a married man—not happily married, but married. I just think you should start seeing some young men, that's all."

She tried to smile. "My mother says men are at their best when they're in your dreams."

Mr. Ayala laughed. "My father said the same thing about women. Don't believe everything you hear, Angel."

"Was your wife better in your dreams?"

He didn't smile. "Yes, but so what? Dreams aren't real. Whatever else my wife is, at least she's real."

"I thought you just said you weren't happily married."

"But I didn't say I didn't love my wife. Whoever said love made you happy?"

Angel looked up and said nothing.

"Just forget I said anything," he said.

She nodded. "Well, maybe someday I will dress up."

He put his hands in his pockets. "Just remember there's nothing wrong with enjoying being a woman."

"How would you know?" She looked at him with her cactus eyes.

"OK, Angel, you win. Just forget I mentioned it. You're as tough as I thought you were."

She half-smiled and drove away.

There was only one interesting bouquet of flowers: a dozen red roses arranged like the feathers of a peacock. She noticed the address was near her house, so she saved that one for last. She delivered the other flowers without looking at the cards. People smiled and thanked her. She made a few tips. "Thank you, thank you," she kept repeating to herself, without ever being aware of the fact that she was speaking to herself. She thought about her boss: Antonio. She wondered why she never called him by his first name—she could if she wanted. He was a casual and decent man, handsome in a sort of boyish way, but she didn't want to be his friend. Calling him "Antonio" would have seemed too intimate an act. "Nice man," she said to herself, "still, it's none of his business what I wear. Why should he care? I'm not ashamed of being a woman—I'm not, I'm not." She wrinkled her forehead. "I drive this damn truck and that's all. None of his goddamn business what I look like." She thought of Michael's eyes; her hands trembled at the wheel. "Heaven," she whispered. She did not hear herself.

She read the card that went with the red roses one stop before she reached the address on the envelope: "Maria Elena, I'm sorry. It will never happen again. I promise. I'll do anything you want. Love, Enrique." Oh, God, she thought, another repentant male. That was the most common message of all. "They're always sorry," she laughed. "All they want is more heaven."

She put the card back and drove to Maria Elena's address. She knocked at the door of the huge house. A young woman about her age came to the door. She looked pale and scared. She was wearing a long bathrobe, as if she had been sick in bed.

"Are you Maria Elena?"

"Yes," she said softly.

"These are for you."

"If they're from my husband, I don't want them."

"I don't know who they're from," Angel answered, "I just deliver them."

The woman opened the card and read it. "The son of a bitch!" she yelled. "If that bastard were here right now, I'd chop his dick into little pieces and feed it to the pigeons in the park."

Angel wanted to run, but her feet did not move.

"I can't believe that fucker had the nerve to send me flowers. I hope they cost a fortune. That bastard!" She ripped the card in half and let it drop to the ground. She handed the flowers back to Angel. "You take them. I don't want these damn roses in my house. Keep them—take them home."

"I can't. I'm not supposed to keep flowers that I deliver." Angel stared down at the ground—she didn't want roses that weren't meant for her.

Maria Elena spoke quietly. "You're with 'Paint the World with Roses,' aren't you?"

Angel nodded.

Maria Elena laughed harshly. "I should have known. I know your boss; he's a good friend of my husband's. He probably didn't charge

Enrique a damn cent for these shitty flowers. I hate him. I hate them both! Tell your boss that Maria Elena threw the flowers out—that they weren't worth a shit—and he can tell his good friend, Enrique, that his wife's filing for a divorce. Tell him I don't want the house either. Tell him I'm going to burn it, and I'm going to start with the bed!" She ripped the flowers from Angel's hands and threw them into the front yard. She rolled up the sleeves of her bathrobe and stuck out her arms. "See these bruises? They're from that lovely man who sent those perfect roses. You should see the rest of me. This time I was lucky—he didn't touch my face." Tears ran down her face. "I loved him. I loved him, I loved him, I loved him." She clenched her fist. "No more."

Angel wanted to do something for her, but there was nothing to be done. She watched her cry.

"I hate men. I hate them all. You know what we are? We're ornaments—those of us who were born with a certain look—we're like paintings. I'll be goddamned if I'm going to hang on somebody's wall anymore." She walked back toward Angel. "Here." She handed her a rose. "For you. This is from me. And don't ever get married. Sleep with them if you want, but don't get married. And don't dress up for them either."

Angel touched the rose and smiled. "Thanks. The best tip I've made all day."

Maria Elena smiled at her.

«III»

Angel drives back home slowly. She does not want to talk to her mother tonight. She gets down from the truck and goes inside. Her mother is cooking dinner.

"It smells good, Mom."

Her mother nods with satisfaction. "I was waiting for your phone call to pick you up."

"They let me keep the truck overnight. I have to go in early tomorrow morning."

"It's not a truck, it's a van. You should have called."

"I know. I should have called. And we just call it a truck." Angel wants to scream at her mother. She smiles.

"Where did you get the rose?"

I got it from a man, she wants to yell. A man! "A woman gave it to me. I delivered some roses to her from her husband. She showed me the bruises where he hit her. She's going to divorce him. She threw the flowers away but gave me this one. She told me never to get married."

"Good for her," her mother says. "She's right to leave him. Just remember."

Angel places the rose in a glass of water. She stares at the redness and touches the soft petals. She pictures herself yelling at her mother: "Shut up, shut up, shut up! You had your chance, didn't you, didn't you, Mama? You had your chance and it didn't work out, and don't tell me it was all his fault because I live with you—I know you, Mama, and you're hell. But at least you had a taste of it, didn't you, Mama? Read your newspaper, clean your house, and leave me alone! If I want a man, I'll get one—a damn good one, or don't you think I can get one? You'll see, Mom, you'll see—some day I'll show you all. You and Maria Elena and Carmen and Sharon—all of you had your chance, so just shut the hell up! And if you ever tell me not to get married one more time—just one more time—I swear I'll walk from this house and never come back, never come back, I'll never come back, Mama." She feels clean. She looks at her mother and wants to yell—and never stop yelling. The tears run down her face.

"Angel, honey, what's wrong?" Her mother reaches over and hugs her.

Angel cries for a long time.

"What is it, honey?"

"Nothing, Mama, really. I'm getting my cramps again, that's all. It just hurts."

"I know, Angel. It's hard to be a woman. Let me pour you a little wine. So hard to be a woman."

Angel wipes her tears and says, "Wine sounds nice. Perfect." She drinks her wine and tells her mother she's tired.

"Go to bed, sweetheart. Tomorrow you'll feel better."

Angel puts on her cotton nightgown. She undoes her long braid and her thick, black hair flows over her shoulders as she combs it with her fingers. She lies down on the bed and falls asleep listening to the steady sound of her own breathing.

Angel is dreaming. She is walking through a forest; she is not wearing clothes. The raindrops feel cool on her warm body. She reaches the edge of the forest where a desert begins. In the distance, she sees a church in the middle of the sands. She runs toward it and her hair flies in her face. She smiles at the smell of it. She reaches the church, but there is no door. She looks through the crack and notices that the big room is flooded with red and white roses—fresh, uncut, thornless, smelling of earth—roses. A man with Michael's soft black eyes is watching her. She is not afraid. He is as naked as she is. They smile at each other. She reaches for his hand through the crack. Miraculously, the crack widens and she slips into the room. He reaches for her. Her untouched body reaches back. When his hands finally touch her, his fingers are soft as rose petals. And in the morning, when she wakes, she will not remember her dream.

OBLITERATE THE NIGHT

Dearest Olivia,

Don't really know what to say about all this, except that it's a big mess. Everything's all wrong, always has been, maybe? I can't remember how it was in the beginning, except that I thought you were beautiful. Now that I think of it, I don't think you ever loved me. You know, I loved you a lot in the beginning—as much as I could love anyone. I don't think you married me for the right reasons—look, I don't know anything about us. I can't figure us out, and I'm not going to pretend I have all these deep insights into your psyche. Look, Olivia, I'm not good at playing analyst. You were wrong about me figuring things out—I'm not all that good at it—not when it comes to us, anyway.

You know, last night lying next to you was all I could take. There I was, trying to get to sleep—and your shape was there like a ghost. No, not like a ghost—more like a shadow. So dark, Olivia. Really, I wanted you to disappear. I wanted me to disappear. I almost got up right then and there. I almost woke you up. I almost said: Goodbye, Olivia, keep warm and well-fed. This sucker's walking. I didn't sleep all night.

So I've decided to move out. I can't explain it, nothing works between us anymore—not anything. It isn't true that I didn't want to get closer, but it's too damn hard. You stopped trying. OK, I stopped trying, too. We both did. What the hell difference does it make? The last two years have been the most terrible years of my life—worse than hell. I can't stand it anymore. Another second in this house and I'll explode. Just looking at our wedding picture makes me want to hit someone—maybe you. Maybe I want to hit me! Nothing was ever right. I couldn't resist that you were so beautiful. I didn't know it would be so terrible.

I've taken my clothes. I don't want anything else, except the painting my brother gave us—I've taken it. All the rest of the stuff, you can keep or get rid of. I don't think the whole process of divorce has to be messy. We've both known enough people that have been through all this. Let's split everything in half, lick our wounds, and keep on moving. It's important to keep on moving, Liv. It's a good formula to follow.

A letter isn't the best way to end anything. I know you think I'm a goddamned coward for not having the balls to say this to your face. All right, have it your way.

But I've never liked scenes the way you do. At first, you pretend everything's fine—and then you move in for the kill. I don't want to be around for that, Liv, I just can't handle it.

Look, do what you have to do. Olivia, I don't hate you—it's just that I can't stand being married to you anymore. You're as miserable as I am. Somebody has to play the heavy. I'm doing us both a favor.

Jonathan

Olivia read her husband's letter calmly. She stared at his perfect handwriting: it was all very clear—every single word. "I bet he got *A*'s in penmanship," she said. She placed the letter where she found it, back on the door of the refrigerator, and placed a watermelon magnet over the top of the right-hand corner. It hung there like an unread grocery list. She opened the refrigerator, took out a bottle of white wine her husband had uncorked the night before, and poured herself a glass. His favorite wine, she thought. She took off her blue shoes, stared at her feet through her blue nylons. *It's my feet,* she whispered, *I always had such ugly feet.* She took a sip from her husband's wine and thought a moment. She opened her briefcase and began to go through her papers. She took out her appointment book and shook her head. Damn, not tonight. She moved the phone from the counter and placed it in front of her on the table. *I'll make it ring like it's never rung before.* She pushed the phone buttons and waited for it to ring. She heard the familiar voice on the other end and spoke:

"Karen? I'm glad I caught you. This is Olivia."

"Livie—what's up, honey? I was expecting you to come by the office before you went home. You left some papers on top of your desk—you need me to drop them off on my way home?"

"Well, I'm not exactly calling about that—well, it does have something to do with those papers—well—look—something's come up. I need a favor." For an instant, she wished she had a cigarette. *I'll run out and buy some. Jonathan hated them.*

"Sure, Livie, be glad to help—if I can."

"Are you busy tonight?"

"Funny you should ask. I'm all dressed up—nowhere to go. Eldon canceled our date. You know, if this happens one more time, I'm going to dump that guy. He's either humping someone on the side, or even worse, he's in love with his job." She laughed. "You know, I used to think men were in love with their pricks, but now I think they're in love with being away from women. Why am I telling you all this?—just listen to me—as if you didn't have problems of your own. What was it you were saying?"

Olivia listened patiently, enjoying the chatter of her business partner. Karen was never all business—she didn't like living her life according to categories—Jonathan had never liked her. Olivia could get lost in her chatter for hours—her Texas drawl was like bathing in water. Every morning when she walked into the office, Karen said, "Honey, let's you and me have ourselves a talk—then we can get on with our work. Can't work without a little talk, now can we?"

"Livie, honey, you there?"

"Sorry, for a minute I forgot why I called. Look, I'm supposed to show a house tonight. Actually, they've already seen it once—they really want it. Can you show it for me? I think they just want to get the feel of the place and make sure they didn't miss any flaws—but the house is flawless. The foundation's been checked, no cracks after twenty-five years, and all kinds of old windows to let in the sun. It's perfect. That house is perfect—not like mine. We might even be able to close by the end of the week. Their credit checks out. That paperwork on top of my desk has all the info you'll need."

"Sure, honey, be glad to do it." She hesitated a moment. "Going out tonight with Jonathan?"

"I don't think Jonathan and I will be going out for a long time."

"Are you all right? You sound a little funny."

"Yeah, I'm fine. It's just that I have this headache—and—"

"I know that tone, Livie. Every time something serious happens, you get stoic. You put on this very tight tone, and your words come out sounding perfect—too perfect. Drop it, honey, I'm from Texas—I'm not impressed with good enunciation. I'm your friend, Livie. We go back a long ways, you and me."

"Jonathan's left."

"Jonathan's what?"

"He's left."

"What?"

"Don't make me say it again—and don't act so surprised. You know all about our wonderful marriage."

"Was there a scene?"

"No, there was a note."

"A note? A goddamned note?"

"Karen, you don't have to scream. It doesn't matter."

"What do you mean, it doesn't matter? Of course it matters. That spineless wonder! If I were you, I'd hop in my car and find him wherever he was hiding, skin him alive, and make a throw rug for my entry way."

Olivia burst out laughing, but there was something hollow in her laugh, and she could hear an echo in the room as if Jonathan had emptied out the house. "Is that what you do to your men back in Texas?"

"Back in Texas, men like to have their own way, and that's exactly why I'm not there anymore. But never mind Texas, Livie, and never mind men—it's you I'm thinking about. I'm coming to your house right this minute—you need to be with somebody. It's not good that you're there alone."

"No." Olivia bit her lip. "Karen, what I need is a bath and a good stiff drink. After that, I'm going to bed."

"I think I should stop by just in case."

"Karen, please. I just need some quiet time. Maybe tomorrow—tomorrow, let's have dinner."

Karen was silent a moment. "OK, honey, have it your way—but if you need anything, just call me. I don't care if it's two in the morning—just call. And if it's any consolation, Livie, he's not much of a loss. He was the dullest man I ever set my eyes on. He was nice to look at, I'll give him that, but even the television set was more interesting than that man. First time you met that man, you should've taken his picture, hung it up on your wall, and sent him on his way. Hell, Livie, they're all the same. Really, it's a shame we're not lesbians—"

"Karen!"

"What?"

"Why do you say things like that? You know you don't mean them. I never met a woman who likes men as much as you do."

"Oh, Livie, you got me all wrong. Oh, I do love men. I like sleeping with them—I like the shape of their bodies, the way they smell. But I also like kicking them out in the morning. You don't see me getting married, do you?"

Olivia wanted to ask her if she felt like crying sometimes because everyone was so far away, but Karen was built different than she was. But she was wrong—they weren't all alike—not men, not women— everybody was different. She let Karen go on talking.

"—Listen to me carry on for filth. Look, Livie, I'll call you tonight when I get in. Don't worry about the deal—I can take care of it in my sleep. I'll call."

Olivia smiled to herself. "Thanks Karen, I don't know what I'd do without you. You're a real gem."

"We both are, honey."

She hung up the phone, picked up her husband's letter—her letter—off the refrigerator door, and walked into the bedroom. She placed the letter neatly at the foot of the bed, stepped back, eyed it to make sure it was in the center of the bed, and walked back over and moved it an inch to the right. She looked up and stared at the closet. He didn't even shut the closet door. She stared at the hangers where her husband's shirts had hung.

Jonathan, did I ever tell you I hated your taste in shirts? Blue and white and stripes, blue and white and stripes, and all of them with those button-down collars. Not once in eleven years did you ever buy an interesting shirt—not once. You even wore those goddamned shirts on Saturdays. I'm surprised you took them off your body when you made love. You know, Jonathan, the hangers look much better without your heavy shirts draped over them. They don't look bare, you know, they just look free.

She pulled at her blouse, ripping the buttons off—letting them fly across the room. She wadded up her blouse and threw it at the picture of her husband's parents, happy and white—the whitest people she'd ever known. "You have the most beautiful coloring I've ever seen," his mother had said the first time she'd met her, "Oh, I envy it."

Why didn't you take that goddamned picture?

She grabbed the photograph from the wall, opened the sliding door, and threw it into the back yard. It fell into the snow with a thud. She unzipped her skirt and let it fall to the floor. She tore off the rest of her clothing, piled her clothes in the middle of the room, and sat on top of them as she read her husband's letter to herself. She read it again and again, as if she were trying to memorize a poem.

« II »

She had given her baby a name: Celina. Her mother's name. When she was alone she spoke to her, told her everything about life, about her father, about her grandparents. She would speak to her in Spanish: *"Querida, que no sabes que te adoro? Tu papa era muy bueno y tu abuela era un alma de Dios."* Once she had been sitting in her office at home talking to Celina, and her husband had been watching her.

"Who are you talking to?" he had asked. It had been easy for her to lie to him—he did not speak that language.

"I was talking to my mother," she had told him, "her name was Celina."

"You never talk about her."

"No," she had answered, "but sometimes I like to speak to her. It makes me feel better."

He'd shrugged his shoulders. "Is that healthy?"

"Jonathan, it's cultural. Mexicans speak to the dead."

"It's awfully superstitious," he said, "I thought you said that you'd stopped being Catholic."

"No one ever stops being a Catholic," she wanted to say. "It's silly," she said, "all of us can be silly."

Jonathan smiled, shook his head, and walked out of the room.

« III »

Jonathan had wanted a baby. "The house is exactly like we want it. We have everything, Liv—don't you think it's time?" His voice was sure, friendly, analytical. He had added up the formula and had come out with the correct answer. Olivia, without even knowing it, had come to detest his reasoning. *Isn't it time?* I'm hungry = it's time to eat. The couch is worn out = let's go to the best furniture store in town and buy a new one. I need a new car = let's buy a Mercedes. We've been married six years, have built ourselves a new house, have fashioned ourselves into financial successes = let's have a baby. His logic was faultless. She sneered at his predictability. But hadn't she thought like him, too? Hadn't she?

She nodded. "Yes, I think it's time."

After two years of trying to have a baby (*it's not like making love,* she thought), there was no baby. Having sex did not add up to having babies. The different positions did not add up to anything. Jonathan urged her to go to her doctor.

"Maybe something's wrong," he said. Olivia filled in the rest of the sentence: *with me.* Why does it have to be me? she thought. *Maybe it's you, Jonathan. You go to a doctor.*

"I'll go," she said. Maybe he was right. Maybe the abortion had done something to her body. Her doctor knew about her abortion, but she told her doctor again. "Could it have screwed up my body? My husband doesn't know—it wasn't his. I didn't even know him at the time."

"You think you should tell him?"

"Obviously not."

"Well, there's nothing physically wrong with you. You're in good shape, in perfect health. Perfect. There's nothing at all that would prevent you from having a baby. Sometimes, it just takes a little time. And then there's always your husband—there's two of you, you know? Why don't you tell your husband to have himself checked out? Some men are infertile—it's not always the woman." The doctor smiled. "They think it's always us, poor devils. It hurts their pride." She combed her hair back and smiled at Olivia.

Olivia laughed. "He comes from a long line of successful lawyers. It would kill him to think he was the end of the line."

"What about you?"

It's nice that she asks, Olivia thought. "Me, Doctor? Well, I come from a long line of farm workers. I don't think I'll mourn the end of that line."

Her doctor smiled, serious and warm. "Tell your husband to have himself checked out."

"Yes, I'll tell him." She went back to her office, and that night, when she went home, she did not tell him. She never told him. She said to him with that dark and calm look of hers, that look which was never calm but only looked calm, she told him with that look that hid: "I can't have—*can't have* children."

"Are they sure?" he asked. There was disappointment in his expression, but he did not say he was disappointed or sad, and he did not ask her if she was sad.

"They're sure." But she knew it was him. She liked knowing it was him. That knowledge gave her something that resembled power, that resembled comfort. "In perfect health," she repeated to herself, "perfect."

Two years later, for whatever reason (they had ceased discussing their lives with each other), Jonathan had gone to his doctor for a check-up. While he was there, he decided to have some tests run. When his doctor gave him the results, he came home in a rage. "I went to the doctor the other day," he said, barely able to contain his anger. "Today, I went back and got the results for some tests. I can't have children. You lied to me—it was never you—you knew it was me all along—didn't you? Didn't you!" He was yelling, his beautiful face contorted, disfigured. "You've been laughing at me for the last two years—laughing your damn Mexican head off. You knew! You think it's funny, don't you! Goddamn you!" He moved a step closer to her.

"Don't come any closer," she said. Her voice stayed calm, not a hint of fear in it. She grabbed the phone. "I'll break this damn phone over your head. I'll make it ring like it's never rung before."

Jonathan slumped down on a chair.

"And don't ever refer to my head as being Mexican. True as it may be, Jonathan, I don't like the way you said it. I've never made references to your gringo mentality."

"Why should you? I thought my 'gringo mentality' was why you married me."

"I haven't a clue as to why I married you."

He said nothing. He was quiet for a long time. "You knew," he said.

"Yes," she nodded, "I knew. And I'll tell you something else, Jonathan, it wouldn't have mattered if you had found out two years ago or today—"

"Oh, yes, it would have mattered! My wife doesn't tell me the truth. Instead, I have to go to a doctor—a perfect stranger—to tell me the truth about my life."

"The truth about your life, Jonathan? No doctor can tell you the truth about your life." She took in a deep breath and looked at him. "All right, I should have told you. I should have told you. You think I've been laughing at you for the last two years? Ha! I haven't laughed for years. Two years ago or today—it doesn't matter—you would still have blamed me. When I told you it was me—and you thought it was me—did you comfort me? I knew, Jonathan, and I also knew you'd resent me for it. But Jonathan, let's get it straight—I don't give a damn if you're sterile or not. I know how you think: sterile = impotent. But that formula doesn't work. Sterile doesn't mean impotent—it just means you can't produce a baby—and I don't want one. Why do you think I didn't tell you? I didn't tell you because you'd have figured out a way to have one—if not to have one, to get one, to buy one. You'd have figured out a way. You're great about figuring things out. I don't want a baby, Jonathan! And if there's something wrong between me and you, don't blame it on your sperm count. And don't resent me for my fertility—it doesn't mean a damn thing—not to me."

"You knew," Jonathan repeated. The rest of the evening, they sat across from each other, no one moving, no one speaking.

«*IV*»

She sat in the bathtub, and reread the letter. She didn't know what the words said—no—she knew the meaning of each individual word, but she did not know how they added up. One letter = divorce. She laughed. *No, that's not it—that's not it at all. Come back here and fight, damn you! I have a few things to say before you leave. It's not that I want you to stay—it's just that I want you to*—she stopped and took a deep breath. The water was hot, and sweat ran down her face, her salt mixing with the water. "And your shape was there like a ghost," she muttered, "no, not like a ghost, but a shadow." She dipped the letter into the water. She watched the ink run the words together. *He wrote it with his favorite pen, the one his grandfather left him. Nice pen, but the ink runs, dear.* She held the letter at the top corner and clasped it with her thumb and forefinger. She dipped it into the water again and again as if she were washing a shirt—washing his shirts—washing the stripes out of all his shirts. Into the water, out of the water, into the water, out of the water. She let the letter dip in and out until every word was gone, until the letter began to dissolve. She wadded up the pulp in her hand, letting the excess water run down her arm. She tossed the wad into the toilet opposite her. Plunk, like the sound of a small pebble in a lake: that's all it was, she thought, just a tiny insignificant sound that had no meaning at all.

She fell back into the water and let go of her body. She closed her eyes and pretended she was floating in the warmest, calmest ocean in the world. Karen had told her that parts of the Indian Ocean were so warm that it felt like a heated pool. "Like a womb," she'd said. She imagined the blue all around her, blue beneath her, blue above her, nothing but blue as deep as her mother's eyes. But her mother's eyes weren't blue—why should blue remind me of her eyes? *Mama,* she whispered, *Mama, Mama*... She opened her eyes and looked up at the ceiling. She listened to the motions of her body in the water. It was warm here—the ceiling so white. She loved the blankness of the ceiling; she could put anything up there she wanted; she could imagine anything, and put everything up there with her mind. She looked at the white and put herself up there—on the white—up there along with her daughter. You never saw my face, Celina, but there you are—there—you and I—are. She dressed them both in white. She held the image up on the ceiling for as long as she could. Held it and held it and held it. "That's power," she whispered, "that's real power."

«V»

She rose from the bathtub and rubbed a towel against her skin. She rubbed hard until the towel felt like sandpaper; she rubbed until her skin felt like it might start bleeding. *Go ahead and bleed.* She wrapped an old robe around her thick frame and let her wet black hair fall free. She wanted to crawl out of her skin—it was her skin that was cold—it made others look at her as if she were nothing but skin. It was nothing more than a shell. But people buy books for their covers; people buy books for their titles; people buy books for their coffee tables, for their shelves. People did not buy books to read them. Jonathan had never read her—she was too hard to read. She was cold; she felt numb; she was lost; she refused to surrender herself to what she was holding in. Don't cry—you'll break—you'll never stop—don't cry. She breathed in and out slowly, in and out, until the tears were buried where they could not rise. She felt a calm. She walked from room to room and looked at her house as if it did not belong to her, as if she were in the market for a home and was browsing through a stranger's house.

God, why did I buy this house? Four bedrooms? Why in the hell did I want four bedrooms? I didn't even know what to do with one. In the back bedroom, she stood at the window and stared at the snow. It was almost spring. The snow was ugly this time of year—yellow and dirty—not white at all. In two or three weeks it would begin to melt and vanish. It was almost the color of pale, sick flesh, almost the color of her mother's skin before she died. She grabbed the curtains and pulled at them with all her strength. The curtain rod came tumbling down. See how easily they fall. All that money, and I could tear it down in a second. She took off her robe and wrapped herself in the curtains.

She walked into her office. Her husband had built and designed it for her—one of his many gifts. She had hated him for his gifts, but she had married him for the gifts he could give—of course she had. He was a lawyer and had "business interests" on the side: a handsome, successful W.A.S.P. who had a perfect body—he built it himself—built it day after day in a gym, but his body wasn't real. When she touched it, she almost expected it to feel like hard plastic. His body was built, but not from work, not like her father's solid body carved and molded from years of bending his back in the fields. Everything about Jonathan—everything he produced—seduced the eye. *I hate you, Jonathan, if you only knew how much I hate you. You hated everything I liked; you thought every-one who didn't think like you was pitiable, but you never hid those things, did you, Jon? From the second I met you, I knew exactly what kind of man you were. You never lied to me. You had no heart, but that's what I liked about you, Jonathan, but I hate you anyway. You weren't supposed to be real. Why are you real, Jonathan? You have no right to be.*

She sat down at her desk and remembered how important she felt the first time she sat in the chair. A leather chair and a desk that cost more than all the money she'd ever spent in four years of college. *It's what I wanted.* She opened the bottom drawer and took out the box in which she kept her diaries, old letters, and pictures. She stared at a picture of her mother and tried to remember what she smelled like. Bread, she smelled of bread. *Mama, what am I going to do?* She shuffled through the things in her box, looking for nothing in particular but hoping to find comfort. A record of the past ought to be comforting. No, no, the past is no differ-ent than the present. Who'd said that? Willie had said that. She found herself staring at a postcard of some Indian ruins in the desert, the only thing she'd kept to remind herself that he had been real. Early in their marriage, Jonathan had asked her why she kept that postcard. "Oh, it's just from a former boyfriend," she had said casually. Her heart had jumped, but she had learned to keep her voice steady through its moan-ings. "He was a nice guy—liked to write stories and poetry and play the guitar. I keep it around to remind myself that I was once young and stupid."

"Did he want to marry you?"

"Don't be silly, Jon," she'd laughed, "It was one of those relationships we all had when we were in college."

Jonathan had dropped the subject of the postcard, but she had always resented that he had found out about it. Why did I resent it? He was my husband. Why shouldn't he know—why shouldn't he have known everything?

The postcard didn't say anything important, but it was something she could touch, and it was real to her. It was real like a statue in a church that she could see and she could stare at, and it made her want to believe in God, and made her want to think that holy was real—that it was something more than the simple projections of the poor. The postcard was a nostalgic picture of a ruin, and on the back, in very neat handwriting it said: "On my way west. Oh, Liv, you should see it. You could die under this sky and not mind at all. I think of you. I always think of you." He had not signed it, and she had never heard from him again. She was glad, glad because it would have been harder, taken longer to let go. But now she sat at her desk—a desk she'd fought hard to own, a desk where she sat and earned thousands and thousands of dollars—she sat at her desk and stared at an unsigned postcard that she'd received a week after her twenty-first birthday. Today, she could burn that desk and think nothing, feel nothing, but she could not burn that postcard.

Willie. William Michael Upthegrove. She smiled hearing herself whisper his name. They had been in a literature class together, and she remembered how he enjoyed interrupting the professor with questions too hard to answer. He was always asking questions, and yet he never felt like an interruption. It was not as if he were challenging the authority of the professor—she got the feeling his authority didn't matter a damn to Willie. He was just asking questions, honest questions, questions that mattered to him if to no one else. He was neither threatened nor threatening. She remembered the first day he ever spoke to her—

"You want to go for a cup of coffee? I know a great place—great coffee—and the art is kind of crazy. You might like it."

"I don't drink coffee," she'd said abruptly.

"You don't drink coffee? You know, it's something you have to try." He was sure—absolutely sure—that she was missing out on something essential and necessary.

"It's for adults," she'd said. And then she wanted to run away for admitting without any coaxing whatsoever that she felt she was just a little girl.

"And what are you?" he smiled, "You look pretty adult to me."

"I'm a nineteen-year-old college junior. Does that make me an adult?"

"Absolutely," he'd said. He was absolutely sure of it.

It was strange to her that he was so certain. So certain, and yet how was it that there was a lack of arrogance in his voice, in his tone, in his expression? He said it simply. "My name's Willie," he said, "Willie Upthegrove."

"Yes," she said, "I know. The professor is always calling your name. It's a funny name. And by the way, I don't think the professor likes you very much."

"I'm not in his class to be his friend. Besides, do you really figure he thinks about me very much? And yes, I do have a funny name, but it suits me. I come from a long line of funny names. What's yours?"

"Olivia Garcia."

"That's a funny name, too. You speak Spanish?"

"Yes, I speak Spanish. It's a good language—better than English." She had said it hoping he'd go away. She wanted to tell him that she didn't drink coffee with gringos, that she only went to school with them, that she wanted nothing to do with them—but it wasn't true, and she couldn't bring herself to tell him something that wasn't true. His eyes kept her from lying to him.

"So you want to have some coffee?"

She remembered how he smoked his cigarette, how he talked shyly, almost afraid of his own words, and yet there was something very right about the words he finally chose. He moved from shyness to animation, and she remembered how he moved his hands re-creating the entire scene in the air, and she would have liked to have been the air just then. And how he listened as if what she was saying was important. And yet, she felt he was not at all outgoing, no extrovert at all. He talked because he found it necessary, and when it was not necessary he said nothing. He was so incredibly present—the most present individual she had ever met. *Now* was everything to him; the future meant nothing at all, except that it would come, and he would be there to greet it.

Four weeks later they had gone to a movie, and afterwards they had gone to his studio apartment to have a cup of coffee. They never got to the coffee. It was an accident—she had not thought about having sex—

not with him—it had not crossed her mind, and she was sure he was not preoccupied with thoughts of sex with her, and yet in one moment, they had both crossed a border, crossed that invisible line and entered into a country of touch where speech was useless, where speech was banished, a country where everything was seen through eyes that were closed.

She remembered taking off his glasses, how vulnerable he looked without them, and not even realizing that he was blind without them. He had looked at her with his eternally boyish smile, and she felt there was something sad about his smile, or perhaps it was the curious look of want that made his lips tremble. Was it want? Was it want? She had looked into his clear brown eyes and seen her reflection in them, but saw more than herself. For the first time in her life, she wanted to know what those eyes saw, what those eyes felt, what those eyes knew—they knew so much—she was certain—knew enough to know that the only way to live in the world was to stay calm, always calm, even in fear.

He was afraid, she could see that, but calm despite the feel of her skin. His palms broke out into a sweat as he touched her neck, and when she kissed him, she wanted to lock his body to hers and keep him locked in her until he died of hunger. Nobody had ever touched her with that mixture of innocence and aggression. She felt he wanted to swallow her whole, to destroy her, to hurt her, but she also felt he wanted to please her, to show her she could feel, to show her that touch was as real as any-thing else she'd ever known—as real as the loss of her mother, her father, as real as her ambitions to have a huge house that would be hers, a place. She remembered sometimes running to his tiny studio a few blocks away from the library and opening the door, watching him read a book, and whispering to him as her heart perspired like skin and thumped to cool itself off. Now, she would say, Now. The first time her husband had made love to her, she had wanted to cry with disappointment because his sweat did not smell or taste like Willie's.

He was not the best-looking man she'd ever met—not like Jona-than. Jonathan was molded in the image of a magazine. Willie was not in magazines. "What are you doing with a guy like Willie?" her roommate would ask. All her girlfriends asked her the same question. She knew what they were saying: Honey, you can do better—don't sell yourself short. According to the law of their world she should be dating her physi-cal equal.

"Olivia," her roommate told her one night, "don't you know you're arresting? Jesus Christ! You should be dating the gods."

Olivia laughed, "Stop reading Greek myths." It was all she said in her defense. Willie *is* my physical equal, she wanted to say, but she told them nothing, and what did it matter, what were they to her? They all had real parents and real houses and went home for holidays. She cared nothing for their world. They could never know what she thought, could not even see that Willie was unbearably handsome. He was handsome in his modest way, and to them modesty was alien. Willie was a modest man, never even took off his shirt unless they were in bed. He was almost oblivious to what he looked like, was too busy thinking about the books he was reading and the world that was sad for him. He'd shake a news-paper at her and say, "We're killing ourselves with fossil fuels, Liv," and he'd launch into a speech and shake his head. No, Willie didn't give a damn about what he looked like. He didn't buy expensive clothes, could not afford them, and would not have bought them if he *could* afford them. She liked that he bought most of his clothes at a second-hand store. He had maybe five or six shirts—and a sweater all the time—the same sweatshirt, the same sweater, but he was always so clean. And one of his shirts was purple and his skin looked soft and white against the deep cotton fabric. He wasn't a pretty boy—but he was a boy. But he was a man, too.

There was something of the rebel in him, but unlike most rebels, he did not have the instincts of an exhibitionist. He was exasperatingly private, and most people mistook his quiet for arrogance. He had no patience with institutions—educational or religious. He knew they would not change, and knew, too, that they would not change him. And yet he was moved by her Catholicism, though it was foreign to his stark Protestant upbringing. Before meeting Willie, she had always detested what she felt was the naive niceness of Midwesterners who knew nothing of anyone who wasn't as white as they were. But Willie shattered her prejudice.

She pictured the first time she had undressed him—she had never undressed a man before she met Willie. He was wearing his purple shirt. She remembered his white skin, the whitest skin she'd ever touched, and how smooth he was when she rubbed her palms on his chest.

Olivia dropped the postcard she was clutching in her hand, and reached out to touch something in front of her. But there was nothing there.

She shook her head. She remembered when he had left that small city in the Midwest where they had gone to school. He had no plans. She had hated that about him.

"How can you have no plans, Willie?"

He shook his head. "I'm through with school, Liv."

"What are you going to do with a major in English?"

"What do you mean?" he asked. "Do I have to do something with it? You're talking like a capitalist."

She'd laughed. "I am a capitalist, Willie—a capitalist without any capital."

He'd smiled. "Well, we all are—we can't help it. But does an education equal a job—does it, Liv?"

"Oh, Willie, what are you going to do with your life?"

"Don't worry, Livie, I'm fine. Just relax about my life, OK? When you're rich, I'll write you for money."

He had wanted to marry her, though he had never asked her, but the unasked question was there the last six months they were together. She knew it was there on his tongue. She could taste it when she kissed him, but she never let him ask. He finished his career as a student and decided to head west.

"Why?" she asked him.

"Because I've never seen it, Liv, that's why."

She saw him, walking to his car before he left. He held her for a long time. He stared at her and repeated her name: "Liv, Liv, Liv. This is so sad, Liv. I'm so sad." He spoke clearly and simply, and she had said nothing in the face of his speech. All she remembered was the way he shook his head, and the heaviness in his eyes as she let his hand slip away. She pictured his hands even now. He was not a big man, but his hands were strong, the hands of a worker. She had dreamed of them many times, and now as she sat on her couch, she tried to remember them. She had written about them in her diary. When he left, she knew he would have stayed. She uttered it now: Stay. She laughed at herself. *He had stayed.*

« VI »

She found an entry in her journal. She read her messy handwriting:

> Last night, after Willie left, I sat on the back steps of my apartment house and stared at the trash cans. I'm pregnant, but I couldn't tell him—he would've stayed. I didn't want him to stay— I don't want to be poor with Willie, can't be poor with anybody.

I sat there on the steps, and he was gone, but I talked to him about the baby, and after I told him I saw that he would marry me. But he was gone. He had that great sense of Midwestern decency. How is it, Willie, that you had the kind of heart that would always know to do the right thing? Willie didn't have casual relationships, not with anybody. All his friends—not that he had many—were serious friends. And they were all decent like him, all of them raised in small rural areas or on small farms, and all of them believing in the morality of work, and all of them with sensible, passionate minds.

God, Willie, why did you have to be good? We're not all like that, Willie. Willie, you don't know what it's like to be born poor—not really—like me, Willie. Poor is not a good thing to be. Shit, Willie, how many times did I tell you that being born poor made me angry? You always nodded, and maybe I hated you because you did understand. But you never understood that my children were going to have everything, and I was going to give it to them. Mama died when I was fourteen, Willie. Fourteen and I already had the body of a woman, but I've never felt like one. I cooked for Dad, took care of him, he never spoke. I told you everything, Willie. That kitchen, those three rooms we lived in—they were chewing me up. School, Willie, that's what I lived for. You say things aren't important, Willie, that they're just things. But you didn't know, could never know what it was like to have nothing, but to watch a television that showed you everything. You don't know about that kind of shame. No, Willie, it's better for you to marry someone like you, someone that's moral and decent, who believes in the pleasure of work. You love the land, Willie, but I'll always hate it. Do you know what the land did to my mother and my father, do you know? They worked it all their lives, following the picking seasons—taking me on that awful tour of America. They died with nothing. Mama died saying nothing, Willie, just looking at me. The year I entered college, my father died blessing God in Spanish. And when I buried him, I cursed both my parents for dying—and Willie, I cursed them in English. Willie, I told you these thing, and I don't even know what you heard.

Willie, it started raining after you left. I sat there, my hand still tingling from your touch. It started raining harder, and I had the urge to lie down on the wet grass, so I did. I rolled around in the green and felt like a little girl, the wonder of it, the wonder of everything. But the wonder wasn't good. It was awful. I wanted to be like the grass, wanted the rain to make me grow. I felt the baby inside me, and knew that I would never let it grow.

The entry went on and on for pages, but Olivia could not bear to read another word. She walked over to the fireplace, threw some logs into the empty space, and turned on the gas pipe to light it. So convenient to light a fire this way—no trouble at all. She took her journal, ripped out each page, one by one. Page by single page she threw it into the fire. She thought of jumping in after the pages, not to save them, but to burn with them.

She fought the memory that took her mind. That day, that day when she went to that man who said he was a doctor. It was an awful place, not a doctor's office. It was a closet, that's how she remembered it. She saw herself getting up early from her bed, showering, preparing herself. She dressed herself as if she were on going out on a date—a date with Willie. She stared at herself in the mirror—and she saw herself objectively. Pretty, really, she thought, really very pretty. "Stop it!" she yelled at herself, "Stop! Stop! Stop!" She banged the warm bricks next to the fireplace with her hand until it swelled. "Stop! Go away! Why do you have to remember?" As she banged, she heard Willie's voice saying that memories made us human. "Memories make us, Liv."

"Stop it!" she yelled, "stop it!" And suddenly the memory did stop. The fire burned calmly. The words she'd written in her journal were gone. It was a great and comforting silence. The same silence she had felt after her baby had been taken out.

She was crying now. She was crying and she knew she wouldn't stop, couldn't stop, didn't want to stop. She wanted to drown; it was good to drown in the water that came from within you, that unknown and unknowable ocean that she carried around from birth, the water where her daughter had lived—for a while—the water of her mother, the water of her father's sweat as he worked picking crops, that had made him look shiny and beautiful.

She banged her head on the wall, feeling nothing, again and again flinging herself against the walls of her house as if she wanted to make herself walk through them, make herself a shadow, a ghost, with no body, no flesh, no heart. But she could not make her flesh and bones disappear, and they thudded against the wall. And without knowing it, she wanted to break it, break it, break it, and fall broken and be broken, and be nothing but pieces. She banged herself, kept banging herself against that wall until she fell on the floor sobbing, sobbing, goddamn it, what happened, what's happening, don't know, Jonathan, shit, it was Willie, no, it was me, because I wanted a place and gave everything up to be safe and now am not safe because safe doesn't exist, safe. A place, there is no such thing. Not for me. Not for anyone. She lay silent on the floor for a long time and went to sleep wrapped in her curtains.

« VII »

She woke up and stared up the ceiling, the white ceiling, the white, white ceiling. She could put anything up there she wanted. She had picked the color herself. "I want the whole house white," she'd told Jonathan, "all white." She had painted it herself, had enjoyed erasing the dusty rose living room with three coats of white paint. Three coats, so the previous color would not show through. But she remembered the color, and she knew her paint job had been useless. The color was there again.

She felt a bump on her head. The logs in the fire were burning low now. She raised herself slowly off the floor, threw more logs on the fire, and turned off the light. She noticed she was naked, and felt cold—and yet something about her skin was good to her, and she wanted to shelter it, to protect it. She walked into her bedroom and saw her clothes piled in the middle of the room. She hung them on Jonathan's hangers. She slipped on a robe and tied her hair back. She remembered how her mother had tied back her hair and braided all her dark strands, and tied red and turquoise ribbons so that when she ran her braids looked like the tails of a kite. The smell of her mother entered the room. Bread, yes, that was it. Bread. She walked into the kitchen and found herself looking for yeast. No yeast in the house. She searched for her purse and suddenly she discovered she was in her car driving to the store. She walked down the aisle of the grocery store dressed only in her robe, and the lights all around were good. She found the yeast, found the flour, and paid for her goods at the counter. The woman at the counter asked her if she was all right. "Yes," she said, "I'm fine."

"You look a little beat up. Maybe you should call someone."

"I'm fine," she repeated.

"You know," she said, "my first husband used to—well, you know. Are you sure you're fine?"

"It's not like that," she said.

She put the yeast in warm water, added sugar. She stared at her hands. They were not like her mother's. Her mother's hands had been worn with work. Her hands were perfect—perfect and ugly from the way she had used them. "I can make them like yours, Mama—they were beautiful." She added flour and salt until the dough thickened. She kneaded it. The dough was warm and soft, and the muscles in her arms and hands hurt as she kneaded and kneaded. The tears ran down her face, and she felt clean. She thought of Jonathan and how she had never touched him, how she had never wanted to. She kneaded and kneaded and thought of Willie's white skin, and how she had felt like this dough when he had touched her—and how she had been too afraid to love him because she had wanted a firm place to live, and could not stay with him because she had been afraid that he, too, would die and leave her with no place to live. Jonathan had given her a place, but the place was hollow and empty—but it had not been his fault that she had painted everything in her life white. Now she was alone, but she had always been alone, and her hands in the dough made her feel strong. She had always felt like a little girl, but right then she didn't feel small at all, and she liked the feel of the tears on her face, warm and salty. Water, it was water, and she felt clean and she drank. And it was hers. She stared at her hands and noticed their deep brown color, and she thought it was a nice color to be. She was hungry and she was thirsty, and she wanted to eat and drink.

She placed the kneaded bread near the fireplace. She stared at the ashes. She poured herself a glass of red wine, and she liked the taste of it in her mouth. And she drank. She stared at the bread as it rose—little by little it rose. From the window, she could see that it was beginning to be light. She was sorry for everything, sorry for herself, sorry for Jonathan and for Willie, and for Celina her mother, and for Celina her daughter. She had carried them all within her, and they had become too heavy. What would it be like, she wondered, what would it be like not to carry them around? Would she look different? Would she feel different? Her heart was heavy as a stone, but it was solid and real, not a shadow. She stared out the window. The bread was almost ready to bake. She stared out the window and looked at the dawn, and waited—for the sun—to obliterate the night.

KILL THE POOR

When he moved to California, he told everybody his name was Richard. He didn't like Ricardo, didn't like what it reminded him of: It reminded him of the desert, of drought, of too many years of praying for rain.

He had a small desk in the basement of the stack division at the university library, a desk next to other desks, desks that were cluttered with personal items, but his was not cluttered. His was clean, neat, organized.

He hated listening to the people around him, though he listened more than he talked. But to himself, he talked a great deal. You could tell nothing about him from his desk, except that he was overly neat. In the top drawer he kept a picture of his nieces and nephews. When no one was in the room, he took out the picture and stared at it. Nine of them, all in the picture. The oldest was thirteen. His name was José, and in the picture he was obviously the leader, the heir of everyone's attention.

They were beautiful children, the sons and daughters of his brothers and sisters, and they were loved, loved not merely for themselves but because they had inherited the job of gluing the family together. Without the children, they might all have gone their separate ways, they might have all divorced each other. But they all believed, for whatever reason, that children should be adored, that children were entitled to be worshipped. The only law in their family was that they should never sin against the children. He did not know where this law came from—he only knew it was written and he could not break it.

He did not believe that life would be any better for them than it had been for him or for their parents or grandparents, but he hoped for them, and he spoke to them in the picture, and sometimes he kissed their faces.

« »

Richard pounded the sidewalk with his feet as if to crack the cement with each step. He imagined he was walking on someone's face, anyone's face, everyone's face, anonymous faces—his face, the faces of those he hated, the faces of those he wanted to love. He stomped harder until he could feel blisters forming as he stepped. He was not aware he was causing himself pain—did not know he could have stopped the itching in his feet by simply stepping lightly. If it were in him to scream, he would have shouted loud enough to break his own eardrums, but he was not born with the lungs of a yeller. He hated yellers, hated people who were always yelling about everything, allowing everyone to see their anger. Those kinds of people, he thought, imagined their mouths to be windows without curtains, inviting passers-by to become dentists, to peer in and see everything: the stains, the cavities, the remains of their last meal, the crooked, dirty teeth.

The scream stayed inside him. He had once seen a woman yelling at her husband in a restaurant, and it had made him so uncomfortable, had made him so sick, that he had lost his appetite and left the restaurant. At the time he did not know if he was humiliated because he felt embarrassed for the husband who was being verbally victimized in front of an audience, or if he imagined himself to be her—her—she who was making a show of herself, slinging her ugly feelings at her husband as if they were nothing more than innocent childhood snowballs, as if she had a right to publicly express anything she felt. He continued stomping toward the bowling alley. He thought of the woman he'd seen in that restaurant and imagined her head beneath his feet. He grunted as the rain began to fall. *I hate winter, I hate it I hate it I hate it.*

He was angry with his girlfriend, angry with his roommate, angry with his idiot boss at work, and angry with himself for not telling every pain-in-the-ass person he'd ever met to go drown themselves in polluted rivers. He walked through the doors of the bowling alley, smiled convincingly at the man behind the counter, paid for his Lysol-smelling shoes, and asked for a lane away from the rest of the bowlers.

"I'm sorry, sir," the man said, "the section you want is closed."

"Open it," he said.

"I'm sorry, sir, I can't do that."

"Yes, you can. All you have to do is press a button. Open it."

The man behind the counter opened his mouth, then closed it again. "The lane at the end," he said. Richard dismissed the tone of displeasure in the man's voice. That tone was common and familiar. *Nothing special about his attitude*, he thought, *nothing special at all*.

He chose a heavy black bowling ball, kicked off his shoes and replaced them with the shoes he'd just rented. He wondered how many people had worn these shoes, what diseases they had; it disgusted him that he had to wear shoes someone else had worn. He winced for a second, then instantly forgot his moment of revulsion. He lost himself in the game he had come to play: he did everything with one quick, continuous motion as if he were in a race—*a race he had to win but could not win, and knowing he could not win, he ran it faster not only to forget he could not win, not only to forget that his feet were tired and weak, but to forget that he was even running a race.*

He was not aware, not really aware, that he was doing any of these things, was not even totally aware of where he was. He found himself standing in front of the lane. It stood before him like a gleaming road, hard, impenetrable, straight. He followed the smooth wooden planks with his eyes, and at the end he saw the white pins lined up in perfect rows waiting for him—they existed only for him—waiting for him to knock them down. He looked around, saw where he was, and found himself. This was all there was: him, and the ball, and the pins. All he wanted now was to toss the ball down the lane. He gripped the ball, his fingers already sweating; he stared at the pins, his concentration perfect; he tossed the ball with all his strength—that force of his arm and body sending the ball towards its destination—speeding. He watched the white pins explode and lie dead.

Bowling was his addiction. When he had given up smoking, he had picked up a new habit. "Those cigarettes will kill you," his girlfriend had told him. She had told him and told him and told him. *Yes, they will kill me*, he had agreed, *but they will kill me slowly like the goddamn food we eat*. "It's such an awful habit," she would tell him, "and rude, absolutely rude." *An awful habit*, he'd repeat to himself, *and absolutely rude*. But he had loved that habit, had loved it passionately, had valued it, treasured it, depended on it—and he did not need to explain his passion to himself, why it was there, why it was so large and so necessary. And he did not need to explain it to anyone else. *I can't quit*, is all he would say.

He used to suck the smoke into himself, feel it in his mouth, his throat, his lungs—and then release the smoke into the air, like a censer releasing incense into a church. Release the smoke, release it—and with it, all his anger. Then he would smile. It was good; it was very good.

When he quit, his friends were happy, though he suspected they were happier for themselves than for him. Everyone around him applauded the monumental act of quitting smoking. He felt like a child having been successfully potty-trained: *good boy, Richie, good boy.* He knew they didn't give a damn about his health, that quitting smoking had nothing to do with health and everything to do with stopping something that his friends found socially unacceptable. It was a matter of doing the right thing, the correct thing. It was like reading the right newspaper— and then recycling it. He was repelled by his friends who never smoked, who never drank too much, who exercised five days a week, who held their lives in perfect balance, who were outraged by the racism in South Africa, overjoyed that The Wall had crumbled in Germany, supported the unions in Poland, and recycled everything they bought. They were concerned, these people that he knew, concerned about the earth, concerned about good schools, concerned about the poor. But they knew nothing, knew nothing about the earth, about people who went to bad schools, about the poor—they knew nothing of these things. They all thought he admired them because he said nothing when they spoke. They imagined he was listening closely in order to learn, in order to emulate, to imitate. "Richard's a great guy," he'd heard people say, but he hardly ever spoke to those people. They didn't know. They knew even less than he did—them and their enlightened immaculate moralities that depended on no God and no church.

After he'd been off cigarettes for a year, his girlfriend had thrown a party to celebrate the landmark event. He had wanted to announce at the party that he had decided to start smoking again. The thought of saying it had made him smile through the whole evening. But he did not really want to start smoking again. Other people had nothing at all to do with the fact that he'd given up his great love. He had had his own reasons for quitting. He felt better. He no longer coughed in the morning, and he no longer wanted to be owned by a pack of Camels that dictated to him how he should live his life. He wanted to know that he could give up something and stick to it, to know that he had the strength and the will to do it. But he missed them, missed his wonderful cigarettes, missed blowing out all that anger and watching it float out in front of him in a soft mist toward God or the sky or the sun. Now he just went bowling.

He bowled an entire game without stopping for a rest. He threw ball after ball, watched the pins knock each other down, then threw another ball, heard that cracking sound of heavy wood against heavy wood. He was responsible for that thunder. The score did not matter, though he wrote it down, then threw another ball down the lane. He gripped the ball tight, tossed it as if it were as light as a tennis ball. When the ball hit the pins he nodded: *Yes, fall.* He clenched his fist. *Fall, fall, all fall down.* He waved his fist in the air and opened his palm as the pins fell. *Yes, yes, that's it, baby, that's it.* He bowled line after line until he felt his back relax, until he felt his face loosen. By the second game he was ready to take his time, to keep score, to enjoy the sport.

《 》

Two hours later, Richard walked calmly out of the bowling alley. As he walked down the street, he noticed a newspaper vending machine. *The Examiner*'s headline read: 3RD WAVE OF PLANES SMASHES IRAQI POSITIONS; U.S. JET DOWN. In smaller print he read: *U.S. Officials Praise Attacks as an Overwhelming Success.* And further down, his eyes fell on *Burning Anger on S.F. Streets* in bold letters. He grunted; he didn't much care for the war, he cared even less for the headlines, and the television reports that turned everything into entertainment because someone had decided that hard things like war were all too complex for the simple minds of American viewers. But it was the protesters that bothered him the most. "Burning anger," he muttered. They'd closed down the Bay Bridge, they'd chained themselves to the federal building, they'd laid themselves down in body bags on the streets and refused to move, they'd burned a police car. They'd all marched down the streets carrying signs that said:

> WAR IS INSTITUTIONALIZED MURDER
> NO WAR FOR OIL
> SUPPORT OUR TROOPS: BRING THEM HOME
> WAR KILLS THE POOR: SEND IN THE RICH

The counter-protesters were of the same ilk, them and their flags, and their patriotic bumper stickers, and their T-shirts with flags sewn in sweatshops by non-union labor. The sides they took did not matter to him—he hated their signs, their slogans, their smug attitudes, the anger in their faces they exhibited so freely, an anger they felt they had a right to express. And not only to express it, but to parade it—yes, that was it, that they paraded it—he hated them for that. He stuck a quarter into the machine, took out a newspaper, and walked home. He stepped a little lighter on the pavement, but the heaviness in him never left him long enough to let him enjoy walking.

« »

He sat at his desk in the basement of the library. The phone rang but he did not pick it up until the third ring. "Stack Division, Richard Díaz," he said. He tried to sound as if he had been interrupted from an essential task. He listened to the voice on the other end—another student wanting to know if there was an opening to reshelve books. There was always an opening, it was not the kind of job that anyone kept for very long—who would want to keep it? Day after day, hour after hour, minute after minute of reading call numbers, putting them on book trucks, finding the correct place on the shelf—and after the task was done, there was no sign that a job had been completed, no sign that a laborer had been there in the rows planting books as if they were seeds, no sign at all that a human being had replaced a book with care in order to make it possible for someone to come along and find it, to harvest it, to take it home and consume its words, and then return it to be shelved again, to again be planted by the same anonymous farmer. It was the dullest of cycles: never-ending seasons where the weather was always the same. It was that sameness that Richard saw every day; it was that sameness that he relied upon; it was that sameness that was beginning to kill him, and somehow he knew it was killing him. Only he would never let himself say it: *This is killing me this is killing me this is killing me.* Saying it, he would have to do something else. Saying it, he could not rely on the sameness.

He nodded, spoke into the telephone, asked a few questions: How old, what year in school, what hours could he work? He wrote down his name. "Why don't you come in tomorrow morning, we can do the paper work, and we'll begin your training." He put down the phone and watched one of the students push out a cart full of books ready to be reshelved. He stared at the books waiting to be sorted in the crowded room, hundreds of them, thousands of them—every day, books, books that needed to be cared for, that needed to be repaired, that screamed out to him to be read, but he hated reading, hated reading because the words were bigger than him, wanted to swallow him. They wanted to swallow him.

Today, half the student workers hadn't shown up for work. "God-damn it," he muttered to himself, "they come in when they feel like it." He'd have to sort books himself. "I'm supposed to supervise," he mumbled, "they don't pay me for this." He shook his head, looked at his watch, and decided to take his break. He went up to the fourth floor of the library and sat near the window where he could look out at the day. If only he had an office where he could see that there was a day, that there was sun, that there was something outside. In his office, there was never any weather, never any hint of the seasons; there was only the glare of a fluorescent light so bright that there weren't even any shadows. In the sorting room, it always seemed like it was the same time of day. Down there, twelve at night and twelve noon were the same. The clock did not help him to discover anything about time—not down there, no, not down there, not down there in that basement. As he looked out the window, he wondered what it would be like to dive through it, to break the glass with his body and dive gracefully, beautifully, perfectly, controlling every muscle in his body, and feel the air against his face as he plunged to earth. He saw himself flying through the air in that one perfect dive and as he hit the ground, the earth parted as if it were water, and then he disappeared beneath the surface, and after a long moment of silence, he saw himself reappear—wet and clean. No harm had come to him. The daydream came to him often. He touched the cool glass, smudging it with his fingers.

The section of the library where he sat was empty. The study carrels were empty and peaceful, free of students who left their marks on them. From where he sat he could read graffiti scrawled on the once-smooth wood. With a black magic marker someone had written: FUCK FAG-GOTS. Others had added their own opinions concerning the statement. In red, someone had added: LET'S ROUND 'EM UP. He could see that there were other remarks too small to read from where he was sitting. He got up from his seat and began reading the proclamations on the carrels. It did not matter that he had read most of them already—he could not control himself. He wanted to understand them, though they repelled him. The carrel in the corner said: I'M LONELY. IF YOU'RE A WOMAN, CALL ME. Someone had written beneath it: HOW CAN I CALL YOU, IDIOT, YOU FORGOT TO LEAVE YOUR PHONE NUMBER. Right near it was another message: HE LIED TO ME. HE LIED TO ME TWICE. A voice of concern had replied: DUMP HIM! HE'LL LIE TO YOU AGAIN.

He walked around the room reading all the words, the underground opinions of the students, and in some carrels he found new messages from the previous evening. Someone had spent a good deal of time drawing a large penis, and had written beneath it: IT'S BEAUTIFUL. He knew the picture would generate a good deal of discussion among the university's graffiti writers, and he looked forward to monitoring the situation. He looked at his watch and saw that his break was over. As he was walking out of the study area, he noticed new writing in bold, black letters: KILL THE POOR.

He stared at the letters. What does that mean? Kill the poor—who wrote this? What did he mean? Who were they, the poor? Kill the poor? What did that mean? It was a song, he thought, it was a song by some punk group, yes, that was it—was that all it was, what did the song say? What did it say?

« »

On Tuesday afternoon, Richard took his afternoon break on the second floor. A few students were reading, others were napping, and one was in the corner drinking a Coke. He wanted to grab it from his hand and speak directly into his face: "No food allowed. Can't you read? This is a library, not a movie theater." He stepped up to the youth and asked him to finish his Coke outside, but his voice cracked and he didn't sound as if he were in control.

"Who the fuck are you?" the young man asked him.

"I work here," he said.

"I don't give a shit."

He nodded. "Someone will be here to throw you out in a few minutes—that is, if you don't go on your own accord."

The student got up from his desk and stared at him. "Anybody ever tell you that you talk like a queer? A gestapo queer, that's what you are." He left the carrel with his Coke.

Richard watched him stomp away. A young woman was sitting at a table reading a book. She looked at him and smiled, "Don't worry about him—he's a fascist. Who cares what he thinks?" He smiled back at her. *What's a fascist? What does that mean?* No one ever spoke with words he understood. When he had entered first grade, he had spoken no English, had spoken only Spanish, and he had spent the entire first half of the year watching lips spill out words he couldn't understand. He had made himself forget that language because it had made him feel like he was all alone and stupid, so he had forgotten his Spanish and did not miss it. But now that English was his only tongue, he did not feel any closer to understanding what people said, what people thought, what people meant.

He sat near the window, not a window really but a wall made of thick glass. He stuck out his hand and left his print on the glass. Tomorrow he would return to see if it was still there. He thought of his girlfriend and how he had not called her in three days. "You don't need me," she said the last time they talked, "you seem not to need anyone." "Not true," he'd said, "that isn't true." But she was far, and he was far, too—not only far from her, but from himself, and it seemed he was getting farther every day—every day a little bit farther, until it seemed that his apartment was the basement where he worked. "Don't call me," she said. "When I'm ready *I'll call you.*" He had been waiting for her to call the last two nights, but if she had called he would not have known what to say. He thought of her, he thought of the books that were growing more numerous by the day, he thought of the perfect dive out of the window.

He stared blankly as he sat. He suddenly noticed the big black letters: KILL THE POOR. No, he thought, that was on the fourth floor, not here, not here. Suddenly, he didn't trust himself, he was seeing things, he was farther away than he thought. He bolted from the chair and walked over to the young woman who had spoken to him. "Excuse me," he said, "but what does that say?" He pointed at the letters he'd seen.

"Which of those words don't you understand?" she asked.

He did not respond to her sarcasm. "Just read it for me, will you?"

"Kill the poor," she said, "It says 'kill the poor.'"

"And what does that mean?" he asked.

"It means that someone has a sick sense of humor."

He nodded and walked away.

All week long, he saw the phrase KILL THE POOR all over the library. Someone was writing it everywhere. He took his camera to work on Thursday and photographed each place where the words appeared. Kill the poor, kill the poor, all week long it was kill the poor.

On Friday morning, Richard discovered that someone had put up posters all through the library that said: NO WAR FOR OIL. But someone had undermined the subversive operation by writing in red letters over the poster: 76% OF THE AMERICAN PEOPLE SAY YES TO WAR. DEMOCRACY IS WORKING. Richard's boss told him to walk through the library and take them all down. Richard nodded, and wondered why that was his job. During his lunch break, he watched the student protesters as they marched through campus. Among the faces, he saw his girlfriend, the one who used to be his girlfriend. She was gone now, she hadn't called. He was glad she was a part of the march, though he did not know why he thought it. He was glad she was not carrying a sign calling attention to herself. "Humility," he whispered, "humility is good." One sign read: MARTHA SAYS: NO TO WAR. He was sure he would not like Martha, not because she was against the war, it wasn't the war—it was the sign.

<< >>

Saturday morning, Richard woke and was happy. No work, today no work. He was content to lie in his bed and let his mind wander. Ten years, ten years he'd worked at the library. He'd started as a part-time shelver. Now, he hated his job and hated himself for not quitting. But what would he do? What could he do? Ten years of working there and he had forgotten everything he ever learned, had forgotten his life before entering the library. He had no memory of what he had done before— no, that wasn't true—he did have a memory, but he did not want to think further than ten years back, because then he might hate himself even more than he did already, hate himself more because he would remember that he had had a choice—at least once, and had made the wrong one. But there wasn't any going back, so it was no use to think about it, so it was better to forget. So now he pretended there had been nothing before the library, and there would be nothing after. He liked Saturdays; they made him happy and lazy. Lying there, he thought he would go into the city and drink coffee and watch the people—the people were crazy in the city. He winced at the things they did there, the way they dressed, but he wanted to go and see them.

Before he walked out the door, the phone rang. Let it ring, he thought, but picked it up. He heard the voice on the other end of the phone. It was his brother-in-law—strange that he should call—it was usually his sister who did the calling. "José," the voice said, "he was in a bowling alley—there's been an accident." His brother-in-law's voice paused, and there was a long silence.

"Yes," Richard said, "an accident? José?" He felt his heart begin to beat faster, something was wrong and quiet in his brother-in-law's tone—grief, yes, it was grief. "An accident?" Richard asked.

"Well, not an accident. A man, I don't know, maybe more, not sure, well—he—they—they entered the bowling alley and José was there, and they started shooting—" he stopped.

Richard said nothing, waited, his heart beating as if it were reaching for the picture of José that he kept in his desk.

"He's dead," his brother-in-law said quietly.

"What?" Suddenly, Richard pictured that bowling alley in his home town. He pictured José and men waving guns. He wondered at his brother-in-law's voice. His brother-in-law lived in southern California—how could he know what happened? He wasn't in their home town. How could he know this? Did someone tell him? Did someone call him? Someone called him, Richard thought, someone, who? His brother-in-law was, after all, José's uncle and godfather—why shouldn't someone have called him? Everyone in the family was always calling each other—all the time talking about everything—reminding each other of upcoming birthdays and anniversaries and other family events. That grief in the voice on the other end, a voice who had loved José from the first because he and his wife had not yet had their own, so José had been their own for years. "Are you there, Richard?" the voice asked quietly. "Did you hear me? José, he's—"

"I heard you!" Richard yelled, but he did not know he was yelling, "I'm not deaf. Why are you telling me these things? Why are you saying them? I don't want to talk to you—let me talk to my sister, let me talk to my sister, you liar—I don't want to talk to you." His heart was beating like a drum, and it would not stop, and he did not know what he said to his brother-in-law, but he heard his sister's voice on the other end, his older sister whom he had worshipped as a child, and she was weeping.

"Nooo, nooo," she kept repeating. He could not stand the sound. "They took him away," she kept saying. He pictured his sister and how she held José the day their younger sister had given birth to him. The younger sister had had a child before the older sister, and the older sister had fallen in love with the boy she held in her arms, and always that boy had belonged to her as much as he had belonged to his mother. He did not dare to think of the mother. "They took him away," she said, her voice falling like a piece of Indian pottery in a store, falling, and falling and breaking. She could say nothing else.

"Liar!" he wanted to yell, "Liar!" But he said nothing, said nothing because he knew her pain was solid and real, and he knew she was not a liar, and that his brother-in-law was not a liar either, and that José was dead and he would not come back. But how was it that he could be dead, only thirteen, how could they kill a child? Didn't they know that he was too young to be killed? Shouldn't they have known that? And then his older sister's voice said calmly, "We're taking the next flight out."

"Me, too," he said.

"Then I'll see you at home," she said. Home, he thought, that was how they thought of their parents' house, and suddenly he wondered why that was home. Wasn't where he lived home? Was that town in New Mexico home? Was it? That town where they'd killed our José?

He did not remember hanging up the phone. He did not know what to do—and not knowing what to do, he just sat. He thought of nothing. He picked up the phone and called an airline and ordered a ticket, and packed a few things, and took a shower. In the shower, he began to scream, he began to howl. He hated having a heart because at that moment it had grown large and taken over his entire body, and it felt as if it were going to break his bones and cut his skin. He wept and did not want to stop weeping, never stop weeping, and it didn't matter because no one was watching, no one was seeing him. He scrubbed and scrubbed himself, but he did not feel clean, and after he got out of the shower, he sat in his room and he felt like a little boy and waited for his mother to come in and dress him, but she did not come, and then he remembered that he was a man and his mother did not live here, and that he was supposed to know how to dress himself.

<< >>

José's mother was sitting in the living room when Richard walked into his parents' house. He remembered how she used to sit in that same spot, talking on the phone to her boyfriends. He had always thought of her as a little girl, but at that moment there was nothing of the girl in her. She was beginning to look like their mother. He had nothing to say to her, but she rose from where she was sitting and whispered, "I'm so glad you're here."

"I wish I weren't here," he wanted to say, "I wish none of us were here," but it wasn't necessary to say anything. He looked into his sister's eyes—José had looked so much like her. She looked at him with want, with hunger. He felt she would wear that look of grief for a long time, because her face was now a newspaper, and on it was printed the news that her son had been killed and she would always wear that headline, and nothing could erase it. She dug her face into his shoulder and wept, and he wanted to kill those who had killed, wanted to hurt the men who had hurt our José, who had hurt the woman who was weeping in his arms—the woman who had been a child and had had a child and who had expected that child to have a child, too. He held her, but he knew his arms did not have the kind of strength necessary to comfort her. It was useless to hold her, he thought, his arms could not resurrect—his arms and his legs and his heart were nothing.

His mother walked into the room as he embraced his sister. He looked at her for an instant and saw her face that had known all those losses already, and he felt that she was the future—after losses there would only be more losses. He did not know how she bore it, how she had carried and brought nine children into the world, and how she had cared for them, how she had lost some of them already and how she had taken José as her own, the first grandchild who had meant for her something that he could never know. He wondered how it was that she had not broken under the weight of all of them. He thought of how he had left this place to escape the poverty, and had escaped it, but now was back to a poverty that could not be escaped. *"Me quiero morir,"* his mother said, *"me quiero morir."* The pain of that language dug into him—that language that he had left behind, had refused to speak because it was the language of suffering, and he had not wanted to suffer with the people who spoke it. His mother called him by his name, *Ricardo,* and for an instant he wanted to be Ricardo and not Richard, the Richard he had created, the Richard that was destroying him. *"Me quiero morir,"* his mother repeated.

« »

He read the newspapers, all of them filled with the news of the killings at the bowling alley. He read the names of the murdered. He read his nephew's name and wondered what José felt before the killer had put the gun to his—no, he pushed the thought out of his mind. He drove past the bowling alley that was closed. The big sign said: PRAY FOR THE VICTIMS.

He did not remember very much about the funeral, only that there was a constant flow of people in and out of the house, and as he helped carry his nephew's casket to the grave, he thought only that he could not watch his younger sister, or his mother, or his older sister, the women who knew about children—he could not watch them, and did not want to think about their grief, and though he, too, had loved José, he did not want to think about his grief either, so he thought only of his job at the library. And the night José was buried, he dreamed of the graffiti all over the library—it did not say: KILL THE POOR, but: KILL JOSÉ, and in the dream, he was writing beneath it, "What does this mean? What does this mean?"

Before he returned to California, he drove past the bowling alley, and the sign said: NOW OPEN FOR BUSINESS. He did not know why he stopped in the parking lot, did not know why he entered the building. He stared at the lanes, and thought he would never go bowling again—how that small pleasure had been taken from him, a pleasure that had been more than a pleasure, but a love, yes, a love, and how that small insignificant love would never be replaced. He walked up to the counter and stared at the woman who was working there. "How can you work here?" he asked. "I'd like to burn this place, and I'd like to burn you." He did not even know he said it, and he did not notice her reaction.

He did not remember saying good-bye to his brothers and sisters, nor did he remember saying good-bye to his parents. He remembered nothing—he had lost his capacity for memory, now no longer had a mind, now put his heart away or lost it—and since he could not remember having had a mind nor a heart, he had no idea where to go and look for them.

One day he found himself in the library, staring at the books in the basement. He was back. That day he went through the drawers in his desk. He stared at the photograph of his nephews and nieces, and though no one else was in the basement with all the books, he did not kiss the picture. He emptied all the drawers, throwing everything into the trash. He rubbed his hands together as if he were cold. He placed the picture on his desk. He read the newspaper that was sitting on his boss's desk. The war was over. The first troops were coming home. The war had been successful; parades were being planned. The protesters had been silenced, had been proven wrong. The campus was silent again. He hugged the newspaper and cradled it in his arms. It was time for his break. He went up to the fourth floor with the newspaper in his hand. He sat down in one of the chairs. The student who had called him names was reading a book and taking notes. He looked up at him and sneered. He looked in his backpack and took out a can of Coke. "What are you going to do about it?" he asked.

Ricardo stared at him and smiled, then jumped out of his chair and grabbed the Coke out of the student's hands. He began swatting him with the newspaper, as if he were a fly. The student, no longer belligerent or brave, ran from the desk. "You're fucking crazy, man!" he yelled. The other students looked up from their desks and stared at him. Richard stared back and yelled: "Kill the poor! Kill them all, reproduce them, resurrect them, and then kill them again kill them again and again, kill the poor! Take all these books and use them to beat the people, they're good for that, they're good for that, point them yes yes yes can't you just see it, the great destruction it will be lovely the most beautiful thing we've ever seen and then we'll be safe and then we can walk the streets they'll be safe they'll be clean! They'll be safe oh it's so good to be yelling, I'll yell until I die that way I'll know I'm alive that I've lived that I am."

His screams continued, he was screaming rivers, his words, a downpour after the many years of drought, it was good, this rain, and he continued throwing books onto the floor, looking at the titles and laughing, throwing them into the air like confetti, the students running away.

"Come back here, you bastards!" he yelled, "Come and bathe in these goddamned books and you will be whiter than snow, come and be clean, stick your private parts into them. This is the day we have all been waiting for, the day of knowledge." He dove into the pile of books that he had tossed on the floor and sat among them. He began laughing. He had never known it was this good to laugh. He could laugh like this until it was time to die. He felt himself being dragged to the ground. He heard voices around him, and arms holding him down. He felt the cold handcuffs on his wrists, and something being stuffed in his mouth that kept him from being heard.

ALLIGATOR PARK

In 1984 or maybe 1985, I don't remember the year—the years seem far away to me like they never happened, but they happened, I know they happened. Anyway, whatever year it was, I think 1985, we were living in Tecapan and I heard my mother and father talking about all the rumors—I was always listening to other people's conversations—the rumors about the guerrillas. My mother said there was talk, lots of talk about the guerrillas, and they were assassinating people. My father shook his head like he already knew it. My mother kept talking about how the guerrillas had begun to bother people and how they sometimes took them out of their houses and encouraged them to join up. It was true. They tried, the guerrillas, to convince lots of my friends to fight the government and after a while I didn't see some of them anymore, so I guess some of them did join. I don't know, it's confusing, but I do remember those things. I remember those things. I dream about them sometimes, but I don't know what the dreams mean, but they scare me, and so now I don't pray.

I had a friend of mine—well, not a very good friend, but a friend—and he was my teacher at our school. I liked him real well because he liked my ideas and he was very good to us, but he always seemed a little sad even when he laughed. Me and another friend of mine were talking to him before school one day, and that day six men came into the school courtyard. The men were all covered up and they had handkerchiefs on their faces and all I could see was their eyes, and the eyes weren't old, the eyes were soft. But they had weapons, maybe rifles, maybe guns—I can't remember—and the men shot and killed our teacher right there in front of us. And the teacher was right in the middle, saying something, but I don't remember anymore what he was saying and I guess it doesn't matter because he just fell. It was the first time I ever saw blood, and I saw a lot of it afterwards so now I hate the color red. And the men, the men took some of the students, maybe six of them, all about my age, between ten and fourteen years old because those were the ages of the people who went to our school, and me and my friend, Arturo, ran and hid. What we did was run and hide, and I remember thinking that I was going to be dead like my teacher, so I ran. Arturo was right behind me and all I could think of was bullets and the eyes of the men. We hid in some fields of a farm outside of our town, and we sat there all day until night came and we never said a word.

《 》

Jaime put down the notes he'd taken down that morning. He didn't feel like reading any of it anymore. It bothered him. He thought of Franklin and the distant look on his face when he was telling his story. Jaime had explained to Franklin that political asylum cases weren't easy and that it would take a long time, and the first thing they had to do was write down his story.

"Can't I just tell the judge what I know, what I saw?" Franklin asked.

Jaime tried to explain that everything had to be on paper, and Franklin answered that he couldn't even speak English, much less write it.

"I know," Jaime told him, "that's why you need me. You tell me and I'll write everything down, and then I'll put it into English, and then we'll fix it all up and organize it so it will all make sense."

"None of it makes sense," Franklin said.

Jaime nodded. "We have to pretend it makes perfect sense. We think that way in the United States." Jaime laughed at his own answer. Franklin laughed, too. For different reasons.

"Why is your name Franklin?" Jaime asked.

"That's what my mother named me."

Jaime smiled at his answer. He was only a kid, fifteen years old, and already he had seen everything, but he still didn't know what was behind all the questions. "Yes, I know, but why did she name you that? It doesn't sound like a name from someone who comes from El Salvador. I mean, like my name: Jaime. My parents are Mexican so I have a common Spanish name—but 'Franklin'?"

Franklin nodded his head. "Well, my mother joined this new church in our town, a church the gringos started, and one of the elders said Franklin would be a good name when I was born, so my mother named me Franklin like the elder said. I never went to my mother's church, but I liked my mother—and all I have left of her is the name she gave me." He paused, "If your mother was Mexican, and you were born in the United States, aren't you a U.S. citizen?"

"Yes," Jaime nodded, "I'm a U.S. citizen."

"Do you like that?"

Jaime popped his knuckles. "Yes," he said, "it's very nice."

Franklin smiled and nodded.

Jaime pictured Franklin as he had looked when he let him in that morning. Franklin's dark Indian features impressed him. He carried himself with ease, with grace, not at all with the awkwardness of his age—but when he spoke he almost apologized for speaking. He showed up at the door saying, "But you don't have to help me if you can't—I understand, it's just that someone said you might help me and they gave me your name and told me where you lived." Franklin had apologized several times before he had even walked into the house. Jaime offered him a cup of coffee and watched in amazement as he poured four spoonfuls of sugar into the cup. He looked around the living room and asked, "Are you rich?"

Jaime thought for a minute and said, "Yes, I'm rich. Not rich like the people who own banks, but rich enough." If anybody else had asked that question, he would have laughed.

Franklin was immediately drawn to all the paintings on the walls. Jaime noticed him staring at them and asked him if he liked them.

Franklin nodded. "Yes, I like them. Did you pay a lot of money for them?"

"No, my brother gave them to me. He's an artist."

"Will he teach me how to paint?"

"I'll ask him if you want."

"And how much do you charge for helping me?"

Jaime thought Franklin already knew there was no charge, since whoever told him to come had probably also told him Jaime's services were free. Perhaps he felt better since he asked the question. "Nothing, I don't charge you anything. You just have to come and sign all the papers, and then when we're ready, my wife, who is a lawyer, will represent you in court, and you can both go before the judge and the judge will decide whether you can stay or not. But once we put in your application, you won't have to hide from the *Migra* anymore."

Jaime thought of their morning interview. He looked at the words he'd written on the yellow legal pad. He asked himself why he did this, and why he let people like Franklin interrupt his life. *Is that what this was—an interruption?* He shook his head. He was tired of analyzing himself, and he was sick of other people's insights into his motivations. His mother said he got involved because he was good person—but she was his mother; his friends said he did these "things" because he wasn't working and needed to feel like he was doing something worthwhile; his brother told him he was guilt-ridden; and his sister said he had a need to keep up his leftist image—"you've been building that radical image since you were twelve."

"What does it matter why I do what I do," he said aloud, "when I know I'm going to keep on doing it?" He shook his head in disgust. "They never let any of them stay legally—so what's the use? They get shipped back like unwanted mail." He arched his back and stretched his arms toward the ceiling. "Maybe this time, we'll win. Sometimes asylums are granted. Why shouldn't it be Franklin this time?"

Franklin should be out playing football, he thought, or discovering girls and sex or something like that. He should be doing all those things that fifteen-year-old boys do. Instead, he's hiding from the green vans of the border patrol and coming to perfect strangers asking for help. He looked at the yellow legal pad and reread the first paragraph. He made notes on a separate sheet of paper. "I'll need some dates," he whispered to himself. "I'll have to make him remember the exact year, the maybe's won't do—he's going to have to remember the exact day his teacher was killed." He took a few more notes and then put the pad down. He fixed himself a cup of coffee and stared at his brother's paintings. The colors were soothing: Indian blues. He wished Franklin could live inside one of those paintings and live in peace. "Goddamn it! Why did they have to go and name him Franklin?!" He took a sip of his coffee and fought the urge to have a cigarette. "What in the hell is a Quiché Indian with a gringo name doing in El Paso?"

《 》

When Joanna walked in from work, Jaime had dinner on the table. She kissed him on the cheek and Jaime breathed in her smell. "Looks good," she said. "We even have candles tonight."

Jaime nodded. "Nothing special. Just felt like candles. I got caught up in a few things—we're just having steak and potatoes—and a salad. I didn't feel like cooking. Good old-fashioned gringo food."

She laughed. "I adore gringo food."

"It's cultural," he said, "and we have a new case."

"We do? Who is it this time? Why don't you just to go law school or become a social worker?"

"Do we need the money? If we need the money, I'll go back to school or get a job. But if we don't need the money, forget it."

"It's not the money, Jaime, you're just going to wear me out. I mean—well—never mind. We have enough money. We have plenty of money. No, I don't want you to go back to work—I like coming home to a clean house and a man who does all the shopping—someone who presses all my clothes." She smiled. "Interesting case?"

Jaime nodded as he opened a bottle of Chardonnay. "Another political asylum case."

She shook her head. "I was hoping it was a battered woman's case or something like that. At least we win those. Political asylum cases are virtually unwinnable."

"Not if you're from Cuba."

"Is he or she from Cuba?"

Jaime shook his head.

"I didn't think so. We won't win."

"You're no expert. Immigration law isn't even your field. And besides, we might win this one."

"How many cases have we gone to court with?" She took a sip of wine and nodded. "Good. An excellent selection, *mi amor*." She touched his cheek.

He served the salad. "We've had maybe twelve cases or so."

"Fifteen," she corrected, "which, by the way, makes me at least competent in the field of immigration law—if not an expert."

"Well argued, counselor."

"But back to my point," she continued, "how many of those cases have we actually won?"

"That's not the point, wife. I mean, some of them did get into Canada. And most of them still write to us." His finger flew out and pointed at her.

"So, husband, now we have pen pals." She played with her wine glass. "And put your finger away. You're hopeless, Jaime. You and I both know those good-for-nothing immigration judges don't give a nationally indebted dollar—"

"I like that expression. You just hear that one?"

"I just made it up."

"I bet you're good in a courtroom."

"Can I finish? You always use these tactics when I'm about to make a point you don't like."

"Maybe I should go to law school."

"Stay home and iron." She shook her head. "Those damned judges don't give a damn, Jaime. You know it, and I know it, and anyone who's ever been in their courtrooms knows it. Maybe there've been a couple of good ones—but they got out. To those guys, our clients are just faces, and they shake their pathetically phallic faces at Central Americans as if they really believe the clients are trying to pull a fast one over on them. The law—the law, Jaime—is all screwed up. The judges are appointed, honey, and if they let too many people in, they'll get unappointed." She dug her fork into her salad and tasted it. "Good. You do nice things with salad. How come you never put in any olives?"

"I hate olives. I won't compromise on olives."

"What's his name? I take it he's a man."

"If you want to call a fifteen-year-old a man."

"He's a minor, Jaime?"

"Age doesn't make any difference, does it?"

"It might complicate things."

"Anyway, I guess we'll have to figure something out. I think his parents are dead. I don't know any of the details—we haven't discussed it, but I asked him and he said something about them disappearing, which amounts to the same thing as getting blown away."

Joanna put her fork down. She stared at her empty plate. "Let's skip the steaks," she said. "Did you put them on already?"

Jaime shook his head. "I'll put them back in the refrigerator, but the potatoes are baked. We'll have to eat them."

"Anyway, white wine doesn't go with steak."

"You don't miss a beat, do you?"

"The whole family disappeared?"

Jaime nodded. "The whole lot. Just disappeared. I doubt whether they'll ever show up. He's the only one that's left."

"How convenient." She took a big drink of wine. Jaime poured them both some more. He walked into the kitchen, put the steaks back in the refrigerator, turned off the broiler, and brought in the baked potatoes.

"Franklin thinks I'm not really a man."

"His name's Franklin?"

"His mother belonged to some church started up by some nice Americans, and they thought Franklin would be a nice name."

"Well, if we can't let them stay in our country, we can at least export our names. Why doesn't he think you're a man?"

"I make my wife work for a living while I stay home and do nothing."

"Did you tell him your hands are magic when it comes to cleaning toilet bowls? Did you tell him you could out-iron Beaver Cleaver's mother?"

"He doesn't know who Beaver Cleaver is. Oh, your mother called. She always calls during the day, even though she knows you're at work. She doesn't think I'm a man either."

"Stop it. You know how she is. Very East Coast. She thinks I threw away a brilliant career in Washington just so I could live with *that Hispanic* in El Paso. We've been over this a thousand times. Jaime, you know how she is. Ignore her. And anyway, she thinks the kinds of things you do for other people are very commendable."

"Yes, like a Peace Corps volunteer. Isn't that nice? I can just picture her patting me on the head."

She reached for his hand and squeezed it. "Anyway, I don't care what my mother thinks, and neither do you. And next time she calls I think I'll remind her yet again that it was you who put me through law school—not her. She has amnesia."

"She's an American, isn't she? All Americans have amnesia."

She laughed. "Anyway, Mother would probably think Franklin was a wonderful name for a Salvadoran."

Jaime stared at her and said nothing.

"What?"

"Nothing."

"You're staring at me, Jaime."

"I think a husband should be allowed to stare at his wife."

"Eat your baked potato."

"Wanna go out for a drink tonight?"

"Can't tonight. I have to go back to the office. Big case coming up."

"Ah, honey, there's always a big case."

"I'm sorry, Jaime, but I win those big cases. And it's because I win them that the firm lets me take our cases. The big cheese calls me the *pro bono* queen."

Jaime smiled as he shook his head. "OK—go. I hate it. Only can't we meet for a drink or something when you finish? I haven't been out of the house all day."

"I'll call you from the office. Maybe we can get in a drink if it doesn't get too late."

Jaime kissed Joanna good-bye, put away the dishes after he washed them, and stared at the clean kitchen. "I'm becoming neurotic about clean kitchens," he said to himself. He walked into the living room, put on a Joni Mitchell album and took out the notes he'd taken when Franklin told his story. He'd drawn a line where he'd stopped reading:

« »

Well, anyway, I didn't go back to school for three days because I was afraid. They knew who I was, the guerrillas. I knew they knew because they had forced some of my teachers to tell them, and a messenger from the guerrillas came to my house and nobody answered so he left a note that said if I didn't join them they were going to kill all my family—my three sisters and two little brothers too. They knew all about me. So me and my family moved to another town not far away where my uncle lived and where my father was working. We just left in the middle of the night, and no one knew we were leaving. I remember that night— it was cool and peaceful outside but I felt like I was burning inside, and I wondered if the night would ever be peaceful. It was my mother who first read the note the guerrillas left and she was so worried she couldn't even think. She said maybe she did the wrong thing by leaving the Catholic Church but I don't think it would have made any difference except I'd have a different name, and she was saying crazy things because she was so nervous. She was afraid I would be kidnapped or killed so she sent word to my father that we were going to join him through a relative and we tried to start a new life, but it didn't last. I knew it wouldn't last, but I said nothing.

When we got to the town where we were going and joined my father, he asked if anyone had seen us leave or if we had been followed. My mother told him no one knew except her friend who was her boss at the place where she worked, and later her boss was killed, but I said nothing. They found her mutilated body and I remember hearing my parents talking about it. The guerrillas said the government killed her and the government said the guerrillas killed her and nobody knew anything except that she was dead and my mother was very upset, but she tried to smile when she found out about it because she thought it was the brave thing to do, and I don't know anything else about all that. My father said he was going to find out if I would be able to continue my studies at school without being discovered by the guerrillas. If not, he thought maybe I'd have to go to school in San Salvador. School was important to him. He said I was smart, and that nothing should stop me from going to school.

My father didn't agree with the guerrillas and he was afraid of them, but he thought the government was just as bad—maybe even worse, and though he hardly ever said anything to me I would always hear him talking to my mother and he told her if the government wasn't so corrupt and ugly and violent then there wouldn't be any guerrillas. But he said maybe men were born to kill because he'd heard that in the United States people killed each other all the time, and there wasn't even a war on, but I don't know where he heard all those things because I haven't seen any killings since I've been here but I have seen plenty of fights in the barrios of El Paso.

My father felt the guerrillas were destructive because they ruined crops and did things that hurt a lot of people who just wanted to be left alone and live in peace, but he said the government forced them into all that violence, too. I think my father was confused. "Life is hard enough without all that killing," he said to my mother, "already we live in hell and here they are starting more fires as if we're not hot enough already." Most of the time the guerrillas hurt or killed people they didn't even know and they kidnapped minors like me as recruits and if any parent tried to stop them they threatened them or did something awful to their property. Sometimes they planted mines in the campesinos' land, but there were rumors that the government was doing the same thing and blaming it on the guerrillas—it's impossible to know who was doing what, but what was for sure was that the campesinos' land became worthless because of the mines so things were bad for them. My mother said things would always be bad for the campesinos, and that it would always be that way. I saw people without legs or arms and stuff like that, and all because of the mines. The government kept blaming the guerrillas for every-thing, that's what a friend of mine said, but he said that the gov-ernment never did anything to help the people who were injured, and he said the government just didn't care—my friend hated the government.

And the government, the government was forming Civil Defense Groups which every adult had to belong to—no one had a choice. What the guerrillas did to young men, the government did to older men. Every adult had to stand guard one night a week, and I knew my father didn't like the idea but he knew he couldn't do anything about it so he would just tell my mother that he would do anything to protect his family because he was the kind of man who tried very hard to be good. I knew lots of my friends' fathers who were not like my father. My father was the kind of man who liked to talk to his children and I have this mem-ory of him when he talked to my mother. Sometimes when he talked to her I knew he loved her very much, I could just tell, and my mother—she was kind of nervous about everything—my mother would calm down when he talked to her, and I liked watching my mother when she was listening to my father.

My father told me that the Civil Defense Groups were formed to protect the people in the neighborhoods but, in fact, it was the opposite. The Civil Defense Groups had a list of people that the comandante made up and the comandante had been a member of the guerrillas at one time in his life but they killed his brother or something—for I don't know what reason—so he joined the government and he became worse than the guerrillas ever dreamed of being. The comandante made up a list of people who were to be kidnapped or killed so they could blame the guer-rillas for those kinds of things. I knew some of them might have been guilty of something but most of them were just like you and me. Like my cousin, Chato, who was killed by the Civil Defense Groups. He was about twenty-one, I think, or somewhere around that age. They assassinated him and the real reason they killed him was because he didn't get along with the comandante. So they blamed his death on the guerrillas. I remember my father talking about it, and he said he couldn't do anything about it but he wanted my mother to know the truth so he told her about what was going on. Someone should know the truth, he told her.

My father was very upset about the whole thing because he liked the idea behind the Civil Defense Groups and he hated what it had become. He wanted to quit but he knew if he quit some-thing very serious would happen to our family so he stayed and said nothing.

Once I asked him how the Civil Defense Groups killed people. He looked at me real strange. "I know about it," I told him. "You must never talk about it to anyone," he said. But I told him I wanted to know everything and that I was a man so he should tell me. He nodded and he told me what was done. For example, the first thing they did was poke their eyes with pins, skinned them a little at a time, take off a finger one by one, cut off their legs, sometimes eventually chopping their heads off. Always, they died a hard death. They did this so it would appear that the guerrillas were torturing them for information. And after he told me these things, my father made the sign of the cross and told me that he did not do these things, that he watched because he had to and he pretended it did not bother him. He said to me that God might not forgive him, but he wanted me to forgive him for these things, and I told him that I forgave him. And I felt real bad about this.

《 》

Jaime stopped. That was all they had covered in their first interview. It didn't sound so very different from some of the other cases, but it always made him sick to his stomach. The others had been adults. This was the first time a little kid had come to him. He focused on Franklin's face and remembered he didn't repeat his story with a lot of emotion. The only time he seemed to feel anything at all was when he was trying to jar his memory. He knew that for Franklin the very act of remembering was like cutting himself open with a knife.

Tomorrow he would find out the rest of it. "Jesus," he whispered, "if anyone ever tortured Joanna that way I'd kill them." He laughed to himself. "Right, Jaime, a nice macho thought—whom do you think would kill whom?"

The phone rang. He let it ring three times before answering it. "I'll be done in about half an hour. Wanna meet me for a drink?" Jaime half smiled at the sound of Joanna's voice.

"That would be great."

"Same place?"

"Same place," he said.

"And bring some money—I forgot my purse at home."

"Sure hon," he paused, "Jo—"

"What?"

"Nothing—never mind. I'll see you in half an hour."

He hung up the phone. He thought of Franklin's case. "I hate this—what do I do? Call the cops? They don't come. Bomb the Pentagon—a lovely thought." He hated all of this—not just that it was happening, but that it would keep happening. It would keep happening and happening and happening. "If I had any balls at all, I'd renounce my citizenship— the only moral thing. But where would I go?" Blood and more blood and more blood. The thought entered his mind that he should buy guns and send them to the right people, and then he laughed at the stupidity of the thought. More blood. "But we're not going to lose this case, damn it— not this time."

« »

Franklin rang the door bell a few minutes before nine. "Am I too early?"

"Right on time," Jaime assured him. His notes and legal pad lay on the coffee table waiting for them to begin. Franklin seemed more relaxed sitting on the chair than he had been the day before. Jaime noticed that he looked older than fifteen. His eyes were tired, almost old, as if he never got enough sleep.

"You want some coffee?"

Franklin nodded and again Jaime watched him as he poured four spoonfuls of sugar into the hot coffee.

"You don't drink coffee," Jaime told him, "you drink syrup."

"It takes away the bitterness," Franklin told him.

Jaime picked up the yellow pad, popped his knuckles, and threw a newly opened pack of cigarettes on the coffee table. "Just grab one whenever you want," he said, putting one in his mouth but not lighting it. Franklin nodded and reached for the pack.

"You were telling me about your father and the Civil Defense Groups."

Franklin puffed on his cigarette and nodded. "My father worked nights, did I tell you that? He worked the night shift at this bakery. Anyway, he worked nights because that's when they did most of the baking, and he made great bread. When it was his turn to work for the Civil Defense Group, he had to miss work—which was bad for our family because he didn't get paid for missing work. My father really didn't want to go because he hated doing other people's dirty work and he was tired of all that. But there was no way out for him because he knew too much about what they did, and he knew they would never let him get out of the group because he might say something to the wrong person. He finally decided to stop going. I guess he figured if they killed him, well that was it. My cousin was a good friend of the comandante's, and he came and talked to my father about why he wasn't coming to do his duty. My father told him he wasn't going anymore, but my cousin told him that if he ever told anybody anything about the Civil Defense Group then he wouldn't ever see the sun shine ever again. So my father seemed more at peace, at least for a while. And then that same year…"

Jaime put his hand out for him to slow down. "Wait," Jaime said. He put down the pen, lit the cigarette that was dangling from his mouth, and popped his knuckles.

Franklin stared at the scratch marks on the sheets of paper. "Is that what English looks like when it's written?"

Jaime laughed. "That's not English."

"It doesn't look like Spanish."

"It's a kind of shorthand."

Franklin nodded. "Are you writing down everything I say?"

"Yes, everything. Later, I'll go back over it, read it, and maybe we'll have to put it in some kind of order, but right now I'm writing everything down. Does it bother you?"

"No. Well, yes. Maybe a little. It's strange, it's like all my words, everything I say, is being put to a sheet of paper. It doesn't seem right. Words are supposed to be said, I mean, words on a piece of paper aren't real like what comes out of my mouth."

"I know, but you see, a judge has to read the case over and think about it, you know?"

"It seems he only believes things if he can see them. You think if he sees the words we write down he'll believe me? I'm thinking he won't. If the judges in your country are like the judges in my country, then maybe we should just forget about this. I don't know. You know better than me, I guess, but I've never trusted words that were written down. I like words better when I can hear them instead of see them."

Jaime nodded. "You like music?"

"Yes, I like music. Music is real."

"But music is written down first, and then somebody looks at the music and plays it."

"No. I know a lot of people in El Salvador who can't even read, but they can sing—and they play guitars and flutes made out of wood, and all kinds of other instruments."

"But what about books? Don't you like books?"

"No. I don't think I like books very much. I read them at school. I didn't hate them, but, well, I don't know. They didn't have anything to do with my life, you know? No, I don't think I like books." He pointed to the television. "I like television."

Jaime smiled to himself. So he was a normal fifteen-year-old after all. "Why do you like television?"

"Because it's alive. Not like a book."

Jaime smiled. He wanted to tell him that television was bullshit. "Why is television alive?"

"It's so real that it makes you forget about everything."

"And books?"

"Books make you remember."

"I see," Jaime said.

Franklin was a little puzzled. "Don't you like television?"

"Well, I don't watch it very much. I like to watch the news. Sometimes, when I'm tired I can watch it for a long time."

"So why do you have one if you don't use it all the time?"

Jaime smiled and shrugged his shoulders. He picked up the pad again. Franklin lit another cigarette. "So your father got out of working for the Civil Defense Groups. Then what happened?"

"'Well, sometime in early October, maybe November—anyway, just after my father stopped working with the Civil Defense Groups, the guerrillas attacked their headquarters. All night, they fought a battle, and we could hear everything because their headquarters were only a block away from our house. All night we could hear bullets and yelling, and it all went on until about six in the morning and we stopped trying to sleep. My mother made coffee in the dark, and we sat up listening to the bullets that filled up the night. And my little sister fell asleep on my lap."

"Were you scared?" Jaime was immediately embarrassed by the stupidity of his question, but it was too late to retrieve it.

"No. I don't know why. I should have been scared, I guess. I wasn't scared like when I ran from the school and hid in the fields with my friend. I don't know what I felt. I felt nothing, that's what I felt. My mother whispered that there was no more music in our country, no more dance—just bullets. And then she said something else that I never understood, but I remember it because she sounded tired. She said, 'I'm tired of being a woman. Their war,' she said, 'not ours—not mine.' And I didn't know exactly what she meant, but she did say she hated men, and the only man in the world who was worth anything at all was my father. She sounded like she didn't want to live anymore. We just listened to the sounds of the machine guns till the sun came up, and almost like magic, with the light of the day, the shooting stopped.

"But I remember thinking how quiet it was, like the earth was dead or something. The guerrillas won the battle and killed about eight or nine men from the Civil Defense Groups. That day, the guerrillas began going from house to house looking for young men to join them. When they came to our house, I knew they were going to take me. My father and mother said nothing. There was a group of them, maybe six or so. My father started to say something, but I stopped him. I nodded at them, and looked at my parents for what seemed a long time because I wanted to memorize what they looked like. I wanted to remember them. One of them told me we had to go, and my mother reached over and touched me, and I told her I would remember her touch, and that I would come back—and I left. I never saw them again, and I know they're dead." Franklin bit his lip. His face seemed to turn heavy and still like an immutable stone. "I don't cry anymore, not since that day, because I know when you cry you're beaten—and then it's all over. But I'm telling you that I hate those sons of bitches, and not just the guerrillas, but the goddamned government, too—mostly the government—so now I don't know what to think."

Franklin lit another cigarette, and Jaime stopped taking notes. Jaime said nothing.

"I have to go now," Franklin said. "I don't know if I'll be back. Maybe I will. I have to think."

"I'd like it if you came back," Jaime said. "I can burn this if you want. You can just come and talk or watch television."

Franklin smiled at him. "You're a good man, I think. I've met a lot of good people since I've been here, but I haven't met too many good rich ones. Your eyes look something like my father's. But I don't think you'll ever understand."

Jaime said nothing. He just wanted to make him stay.

"Would you mind very much if I took some of your cigarettes?" Franklin asked. "I don't have any, and I'd like some."

"Take them all," Jaime said.

"Thank you." He got up from the couch and headed for the door.

"I'd like it if you came back," Jaime said.

Franklin nodded and opened the door. "Thank you," he said again. And walked away.

« »

Jaime took a walk that afternoon and thought about his morning visit with Franklin. He sat down on a bench at San Jacinto Plaza and stared at the water coming down from the fountain. He stared at the Mexican tile and shook his head. He remembered the times his grandfather used to bring him here to watch the alligators when he was a little boy. He loved the alligators. But some soldiers from Fort Bliss had gotten crazy-drunk one night, and they killed them—stabbed them, knifed them, cut them up. He hated thinking about the dead alligators, and ever since then he'd never liked soldiers. Those poor alligators never had a chance. His grandfather had tried to console him by telling him that alligators didn't belong in El Paso anyway, and that they'd never been happy outside the swamps where they came from. "But Grandpa," he'd cried, "the poor alligators, the poor, poor alligators—killed by those mean soldiers." He thought of that little boy, and he remembered how the park had changed after that. But the people still gathered here to catch their buses, or eat lunch, or just sit. And no one even remembered the alligators anymore. He noticed a border patrol officer ask a young man for his papers. The young man shook his head and the green uniform took him by the shoulder and led him to the green van. "I hate this damned park," he whispered, and walked back home.

"What, no dinner tonight?" Joanna asked as she walked in the door. "Sorry I'm late. But I have a new client and—well, you know—you've heard it all before."

Jaime nodded. He was sitting in the rocking chair in the living room.

"You look preoccupied," she said.

He nodded.

"Talk to me," she said. "I hate your silences."

He got up from where he was sitting and held her. She said nothing. She gently pushed him back a little and put her hand on his cheek. "I love your eyes," she said. "And tonight they're dark and brooding just like the first time you kissed me."

"It was you who kissed me," he said softly.

"Well, I had to. I was afraid you were never going to get around to it."

"I'm slow," he whispered, "I've always been very slow."

"You want to tell me about it?"

He walked over to the coffee table and sat on the couch. Joanna followed him and sat down next to him. He read her the notes he'd taken from Franklin's two visits.

Joanna listened to his voice, not moving—her eyes glued to her husband's lips. He finished reading Franklin's words and looked at her.

"We'll do everything we can, honey. You know we will."

"It won't be enough."

"So we should bring down the U.S. Government?"

"Yes, we should bring down the U.S. Government."

"Long live the revolution."

"Shh," he said, "let's not talk about it."

He lay down on the couch and pulled her on top of him. "Let's lie here and leave the lights off and pretend the world doesn't exist, and in the morning we'll get up swinging."

They fell asleep in the darkness.

《 》

A week went by without a word from Franklin. Every day, Jaime hoped he would come back. He studied the notes he'd taken so far. He would have to put in the correct dates, the names of all the places. He would have to turn the run-on sentences into cleaner phrases. He would have to take out all the personal asides and make Franklin's story into a document. He would make Franklin's affidavit nice and neat and type it out on nice white paper with a nice IBM typewriter, and the judge would look at it and say, "No."

"It won't happen this time," he repeated, "not this time." He waited for Franklin to return.

One morning Franklin showed up at the door. "I'm going back to El Salvador," he said. "I've decided that I don't want to live here. This isn't my country. I'm going back."

Jaime said nothing. He just looked at Franklin and finally spoke: "But you'll never find your parents."

"I know. That's not why I'm going back. They're dead—I know they're dead."

"And if you go back, you might be dead, too."

"But the judge might not let me stay anyway, and I'd rather go back on my own then be sent back."

"But we don't have to do this the legal way—you can just disappear into a big city and no one will ever find you. There are lots of ways of doing things, Franklin."

"I don't want you to break any laws—not for me, anyway."

"I wouldn't be breaking the law for you, Franklin, I'd be breaking it for me. Do you understand?"

Franklin shook his head. "No. But it doesn't matter. You don't understand me either. But I want you to know that *I am* going back. I don't know what there is for me in my country, but it is my country, and I'm returning."

"So why did you come back to see me?"

"Because I wanted to finish telling you my story. I never finished telling you everything. I don't think that's right. I don't like being told half a story. When I was little, my grandmother used to tell me stories, but she was old and she'd forget sometimes and never finish telling me the story—I hated that because I was always left wondering what happened. It doesn't seem right to begin something and then never finish. I want to finish, but I don't want you to write it down. I just want to tell you."

Jaime nodded.

"Where's my cigarettes?" Franklin asked.

Jaime laughed and pulled the pack from his shirt pocket and handed them to him.

"So anyway," he said lighting his cigarette, "I was telling you how the guerrillas took me from my parents. I didn't know where they were taking us. I remember we stopped to rest about six hours after we left our village in a place I didn't recognize, but then I really didn't know very much about the different places in El Salvador because I never went anywhere, except one time I went to San Salvador with my father. So we took a short rest and we kept walking until it got to be night and finally we rested. They didn't give us anything to eat, but I did get a glass of water which tasted good. I still remember that.

"The next day they explained to us why they had taken us. It was sort of like a class at school. The leader, a comandante, seemed like a nice man—he didn't talk like a killer. He talked more like a poet, I think. I bet he could sing, and I bet he even played the guitar, at least that's what I thought at the time. So he explained things to us and we all listened. One person asked what the fight was about, and he told us we would discover that in the future, but I never have figured it out. I don't think even today that I have it all straight in my head. It's strange. Maybe I'm not as smart as my father thought I was, or maybe I'm smart but I didn't go to school long enough to be able to figure out all these things—but anyway, that future the comandante spoke about never came.

"They said they would arm us with weapons when we were ready. They told us that it was our duty to fight, and that we should be very proud to have the honor of fighting with them because they were fighting for the freedom of our people. He asked if any of us had ever joined the government forces, which was a dumb question because if any of us ever had, we weren't going to tell them, and anyway we weren't old enough. He explained that if we ever betrayed them, either we would be killed or our families would be slaughtered like pigs.

"I thought about my teacher. If you asked too many questions they would take you to a place called Calaveras, which was a cave—at least that's what I heard—a cave where you were punished and I heard people talk about it. Later, I learned that the government liked to place spies in with the guerrillas, so everybody was kind of paranoid. There was lots of spying going on, and lots of betrayals all over the place.

"During our training, we had to learn how to use the particular gun or rifle or machine gun they gave us. Everyone had to learn how to use a weapon. I guess our training was pretty much like that of any military organization—they gave you orders and you followed them, and they talked about the enemy and everybody became like brothers. And maybe, I think, it was all a big lie—or am I wrong?"

Jaime nodded. "Are you sure you're just fifteen?"

"Well, I'm going to be sixteen soon," he said seriously, "and maybe I'll think about getting married like you."

"That's crazy, Franklin. Why would you want to get married?"

"Well, marriage is a good thing, isn't it?"

"Maybe. I didn't really want to get married—it's just that I wasn't stupid enough to let the best woman I ever met leave me. I married her because I loved her, not because I decided that I was supposed to get married. Do you see the difference?"

Franklin nodded, but Jaime didn't think he got the message. "Your wife must love you very much, otherwise she wouldn't support you."

Jaime laughed. "She does."

Franklin thought a minute. "Well, see, I don't have a family any-more, so I guess I'm just going to have to start a new one."

Jaime nodded. It was a bad idea, he thought, but it was hard to argue with Franklin's logic.

Franklin lit another cigarette. "Can I finish the story?"

Jaime nodded.

"The first time I was involved in a battle was when we were travel-ing to some place they called Primavera. We were resting when we were discovered by the military, so we fought. It was the first time I fired a rifle at a human being and I don't think I hit anyone, but I can't say for sure. About ten guerrillas were killed and three soldiers died stepping on mines. We fled towards the hills, and my ears were ringing like bells from the gun shots. The sound of bullets is a funny thing—it becomes some-thing like a game. I don't know what made me think of that at the time, but that's what I thought. You lose yourself in the whole thing, like when you're a kid and nothing exists but the game you're playing, you know?

"Another time, we were near this place called Las Piedras when a plane was spying in the sky, and they discovered our camp where we were training. We were training new recruits—they were young like me. I called them 'the stolen,' and all of a sudden we were being hit from all sides. Out of the hundred and fifty of us, about fifty of us were killed. I remember seeing leaves soaked in blood and wanting to throw up. We took the wounded with us to a clandestine hospital and many of them had to have their arms or legs amputated. The hospital was in a big underground foxhole and it was big enough to hold about thirty people. We had a few people who knew something about medicine, and a doc-tor, at least I guess he was a doctor. We left the wounded there, the rest of us had to move on. We just left them there. Two weeks later we returned, and most of the wounded were dead. We made graves and buried them. I hated that. I wanted to jump in those graves, too. I knew I wasn't alive anymore. No, I wasn't alive.

"Sometimes we used to engage in small battles lasting about two or three hours with the military. Sometimes we'd set up traps and ambush the military and escape into rural areas, but we moved around a lot. It wasn't good to stay in one place.

"About a month after I thought of jumping into all the graves, I decided I would escape from the guerrillas. It wasn't that I didn't like the men I was fighting with. I liked them. I don't know, I just didn't belong there. So one night we set up camp after having stolen some supplies and for once we had good food, or at least decent food, and I knew this was the night, the night I would escape, because I knew it was my turn to stand guard. There were three of us who decided to escape, but only two of us were scheduled to be on guard, so the third guy traded shifts with another guy as we ate supper. And we were ready. At about two in the morning, when everyone was asleep, we just took off, but someone had been keeping an eye on us and followed us. When he figured out we were betraying the cause, he started shooting at us in the dark and we ran, but only two of us made it. The guy that was hit just yelled, 'Run! Run!' and that was the last thing he said. Last week, a bunch of us were playing soccer in an alley-way and somebody yelled at the guy with the ball: 'Run! Run!' and all of a sudden I got dizzy and had to drop out of the game. I got a friend of mine to buy me some beer, and I got drunk for the first time in my life."

He lit another cigarette and his hands were shaking. "So I made my way back to my village, and when I got back to my house, the house was empty. I went to the bakery where my father worked, and my father's boss looked at me strangely and took me into his house above the bakery. He said I should leave. He told me in a mean voice that my parents were gone—that they disappeared and they would never be seen again. He said that he had been harassed and that he was in deep trouble—all because of my father. He said now that things were settling down he didn't want any more of all this trouble so I should just go. He was yelling. I stared at him and started to walk out. He grabbed me by the shoulders. 'Wait,' he said. I thought he was going to hit me, so I got away from him. He came at me, so I raised my hands to cover my face. Then he just said real quietly, 'Stay here until night. I know someone who will take you to San Salvador. My son—my son will take you.' I waited there until night, and before I left, the man put some money in my pocket—it was a lot—and he said, 'Your father—your father—he was my friend, and I'm running out of friends. Go. Leave this country—just go, and don't ever come back.'

"The baker's son took me to San Salvador and told me I should go to a certain house and they would let me live there until I decided what to do. I was there for a month, and one day in the streets of San Salvador I saw one of the guerrillas—one of the trainers—he saw me, too. I just ran. He ran after me, but I finally lost him. I knew then that I had to leave. The baker had given me enough money to leave the country, so I began making plans. I stopped going out, and two days later the baker's son turned up at the house and said the Civil Defense Groups had burned down his father's bakery and taken his father. He said he had also gotten a notice that he must now join the military, but he said, 'I won't kill my own people.' I told him all about what happened to me, and the next day we left for the United States.

"So here I am. I thought that when I got here I would be free, but I wasn't thinking right. I'm not free—don't belong here—I don't feel right. This is your country, not mine, and I don't think it could ever be mine. Look at me, does it look like I belong here?"

"All of us come from different places, Franklin, all of us. My parents came from Mexico with their parents when they were small. And now they belong here."

"Mexico isn't fighting a war. I'm going back. If I stay here, I'll die—at least that's how I feel. If I have to feel dead, I'd rather feel dead in my own country."

"But you're only fifteen, Franklin—"

Franklin laughed. "I know you think I'm just a kid, but I'm not."

Jaime nodded slowly. "How will you get back?"

Franklin shrugged his shoulders. "If I got here, it will be even easier to get back."

"Can I help you? Maybe I can take you. I have a car—I could take you back."

"No. You belong here with your wife. You don't belong in my country." Franklin shook Jaime's hand and started to leave. "I'm glad I got to talk to you," he said. "It was good for me to talk."

"Will you write to me when you get back?"

"If you want me to."

Jaime wrote down his address and handed it to him. He walked over to a clay jar where he kept some cash. He reached into his wallet and took out all the money in it. "Take this," he said, "you'll need it."

Franklin did not reach for the money.

"Please take it."

Franklin nodded.

Jaime tried to smile. "Write to me. Let me know you're all right."

Franklin touched Jaime's shoulder and left.

《 》

Franklin wrote to Jaime when he got back to El Salvador. Jaime wrote back, and they continued to write to each other for almost a year. Jaime sent him a present for his sixteenth birthday. Soon after, Franklin stopped writing. Jaime sent three letters in a row without a response. He almost decided to go to El Salvador and look for him, but he thought about what Franklin had said: "You don't belong in my country." He re-read all of Franklin's letters and thought about how Franklin might have become a poet because of the way he saw things. He discovered that Franklin mentioned the names of the people he was living with. He wrote to them and asked them about Franklin. He finally got a letter from them telling him that Franklin had disappeared, but they had hopes that he was still alive. Jaime knew he wasn't.

Jaime called Joanna on the phone after he read the letter and asked her to meet him at Alligator Park.

"Where?" she asked.

"Alligator Park. You know, San Jacinto Plaza."

"I've never heard anyone call it that before. Why do they call it that?"

"They used to keep alligators there, but some drunk soldiers ripped their guts open. Just meet me there."

When Joanna got to the park, she found her husband sitting on one of the benches. She knew that look of his.

"I got a letter today," Jaime said. "Franklin's disappeared." He clenched a fist. "Somebody mistook him for an alligator."

Joanna held on to his wrist until he unclenched his fist. She slipped her hand into his open palm. They sat in the park saying nothing all afternoon—the ghosts of the dead all around them.

In memory of those who died

IN LONDON THERE IS NO SUMMER

Lizzie and I took our days off together. Often we would buy bread and cheese and walk down Finchley Road into the West End. The walk from Kilbourn was far, but it never mattered. We wanted to see everything. We liked going to St. James Park and listen to the music. Sometimes, there was a band playing even though it was raining, and the band members looked ridiculous, sitting in the rain getting soaked, looking very intent and pretending the rain didn't exist. They played to the tourists and to the ducks.

I don't remember most of the things we talked about. I knew that she was the youngest child in her family and that her father was a Notre Dame football fan. She'd spent a year in Ireland, and when the summer was over she was going back to Chicago. I also knew that most of what we said was in the seconds of silence between the words we were uttering, and even though London was very wet that summer, when I was with her, I was very dry. Neither one of us noticed that London summers didn't exist. We went to see Marcel Marceau one evening. I remember how clean she smelled that night. Not at all like London.

Once, when we took a day off, I met her at the soup kitchen where she lived. The place was run-down and ugly and dull like the weather. Everywhere there was peeling paint in a neighborhood full of squats, but that day it felt good. The neighborhood felt good. She'd bought a cheese-cake because she knew I liked it, and we drank coffee and tried to decide what we could do that day that didn't cost money. We wound up not going anywhere, but the coffee was good, and the talk was good, and the weather didn't seem so bad. She told me about her year in Ireland. I could picture her against the green hills. I told her about my family, about my childhood. I told her everything I could think of. She wondered if I missed the desert. I told her I missed my people. She asked what it was like to be a Chicano. I thought it was a funny question, but I told her it was a little like living in a home for the homeless. It was a stupid thing to say. It wasn't like that at all. I would never be homeless: I had the desert. London wasn't the desert. Well, it was a desert, but not the kind of desert that would ever be any kind of home—not for me. Not for her. She wanted to know why I wanted to become a priest. I don't remember what I said, but I'm sure whatever I said, I believed it.

He stopped reading for a minute. Whatever I said, I don't believe it anymore. I don't believe a lot of things anymore. He didn't want to think about it. He kept reading the journal.

I talked and talked for a long time. She looked at me with her gray eyes, and even though they were very gray, I thought they were very blue. She asked me if she could touch me. I didn't say anything.

I put my hand on her face and touched her freckles.

≪ ≫

Sister Susana Marie looked him over carefully as if she were inspecting a novice entering a convent. There was no hint of what was going through her mind as she looked at the young man before her. She could have made a fortune playing poker. She stared straight into his face. "You look to me to be a bit fragile."

Standing out in the London drizzle, the youth smiled at her, his nervousness like a line of electricity running through his face. "I only look fragile to people who don't know me, Sister."

She was surprised by his remark, and laughed despite herself. "Come in. I am afraid the rain is not very welcoming, Michael."

"Miguel," he corrected, "my name is Miguel."

She pretended not to hear his correction. She took his coat and hung it on a rack next to the door. The house was dark and clean, and the young man fought the urge not to go back out into the rain. "I have been expecting you. I received all your letters and was very impressed by the frankness of your words. Your face is rather soft for such strong handwriting." He might have been insulted, except that somehow he sensed she meant no harm. Her way was hard. He had known many like her. He smiled at the way she spoke. She sounded oddly formal, perhaps because she did not use contractions. She spoke in full sentences.

She led him to the second floor where he'd be staying. On the way up the stairs, he felt as if he were going to be sick, and he felt hollow as he heard his feet on the wood floor. *Maybe I'm not here, maybe I've left my body, maybe it's not my feet I hear hitting the floor.* But as soon as he reached the top of the stairs, he felt alive again, felt he was back in his body. It was his feet touching the wood floor, *his.* He noticed Sister Susana Marie's walk, confident and overwhelming. Her steps were anything but delicate, as if she deliberately wanted to remind the floor that it existed only to be stepped on. The room she showed him was small, long and narrow, like a closet with two bunk beds squeezed into it. "You will be living here with Tim, Andrew, Patrick, and Father Richard."

"That's a lot of roommates," he said.

She looked at him sharply. "If you don't like people, then you have come to the wrong place."

"No," he smiled, "people are good. I never met a man I didn't like. And for that matter, I never met a woman I didn't like."

"I am not sure how to take you," she said. "Well, I suppose if you are here, you must be decent. Perhaps I was expecting you to be like your friend who recommended you."

"George."

"Yes, George was as calm as the ocean. You are not like him. You are not calm. Perhaps you will learn to be at peace while you are here."

"If I wanted to know peace," he said to himself, "I would not have come here." He nodded at her. "Maybe you're right, Sister, but I can't be all bad. I mean, George and I are good friends."

"Well, I can see how you might be drawn to him. Perhaps he has something you need."

"Perhaps it was him who was drawn *to me.*"

"Of course," she smiled, "that is a possibility, isn't it?"

His nervousness left him as he spoke to her. He had a feeling that they would fight all summer. He found the thought comforting. He wondered if he would have time to settle in before his job began—whatever that was. There was a moment of quiet between them. He was about to ask if he could have some time alone, when she interrupted him. She would always be one step ahead of him.

"I want you to take extra time with Father Richard. He is a priest who has come to work from Chile. Perhaps he will start a home for homeless men in his own country after his experience with us. At least that is my hope. But his English is very poor. In your letter, you mentioned that you spoke Spanish. You must help him." She straightened out the blankets on one of the beds. "Tim does not know how to make a bed. I must speak to him again." She looked at him and shook her head. "There are only four beds, but one of you can take the floor. You are young, Miguel, and even if you are fragile, the floor will be good for your back."

"It'll be a bit crowded," he said.

"Yes, but you have a window, and on a good day you can see the sky."

"What sky?" he muttered.

She didn't hear him, but she saw the look on his face and shook her head. "Did you come to work with the poor or did you come on holiday?"

"I came to work with the poor, but—"

"Then you live like the poor," she said, interrupting him.

He had wanted to say that he had never equated living in a closet with working with the poor. He just nodded.

"Good," she said, "there is one of our men who needs a bath."

She took his backpack and put it on the floor of the room. "You travel lightly. That is a very good sign."

She led him to the bathroom on the third floor. "The gentleman in the bathtub needs a good cleaning, poor chap. You must be firm. Sometimes he gets angry. If he is in bad spirits, you must not let him treat you badly, but you must not treat him badly, either. Remember, he is Christ. And when you finish, you must go to the kitchen to help Tim with dinner. I am sure you will find it. The kitchen is in the basement." She left him standing at the bathroom door, and he stared at it, not wanting to enter, not wanting to see her Christ.

He pushed the door open and walked into the bathroom that smelled of pine oil and cigarettes, years and years, layer upon layer of stale smoke and cleanser—never to be clean, never to smell clean. The smells only served as reminders of the futile attempts, the lost labors wasted in this room. He looked at the man in the tub, who looked back at him with half-dead eyes. The man said nothing. Miguel studied him as if he were a painting on the wall, as if he were not real. The man looked old to him, almost old enough to be the original owner of this Victorian house in decline. He had scabs on his thin legs, a scar across his chest where someone had dug in a knife as if he were a piece of wood to be carved, scratches on his face, faded tatoos on his arms, eyes that seemed to see nothing. His eyes and skin were colorless. And wrinkles, loose skin on crooked bones. He looked up at Miguel and seemed glad to wait until he was ready. If I were in his place, Miguel thought, I would be humiliated, but later he was to think that most of the men who lived in this place were too broken to feel that kind of shame. At the end of the summer, he would write in his journal: *Perhaps it is a freedom to be unashamed of what you are—whatever that may be.*

The man just sat there and said nothing. Miguel waited and wanted to smoke a cigarette. He wanted to do anything but touch him. He knelt on the floor, found the soap and towel, and began to wash his body. The body in the tub mumbled. He lifted the man's leg slowly and washed his foot carefully. *You must be gentle.* But it seemed to him that this man's body had known nothing but violence, and he doubted that he could recognize gentleness. He washed the man's body inch by inch, taking all the time he needed. The man in the tub was patient, almost as if he knew Miguel was afraid of adding another mark, another scar, or afraid that one of his marks would stick to his hands. He washed the man's gray hair and rinsed it with a pitcher. The man closed his eyes and breathed in deeply.

"All done," Miguel said.

"Will you be helping me up?" the man asked, his voice inexplicably young and clear.

"Yes," Miguel said. He helped him out of the tub and gave him a towel.

"You new here?" the man asked.

"Yes."

"We get young chaps all the time. They come to help the Sisters. I'm not Catholic meself. Don't think God thinks much of me neither. But the Sisters aren't bad birds—a bloody pain in the ass sometimes, but they're women. What d'ya expect from women?"

Miguel nodded and smiled.

"Young blokes like you, they come and go. Most of them not as young as you, though. You look like you're just a lad. How old?"

"Twenty-three. You?"

"Forty," he said, "be forty-one next month."

Forty. Miguel stared at him. The man stared back with his colorless eyes. Miguel noticed they were a tired blue. "Sorry," he said, "I didn't mean to stare."

"It's all right. I'm used to it. I look older, I know. Lived on the street most of me life. Life will be better for you. Your Catholic God won't spit at you like he spit at me. Twenty-three are you? Don't look a day older than sixteen. I got a pound in me pocket that says you're still a virgin."

Miguel laughed. "You lose, but keep the pound."

"You lie." The man smiled. His teeth looked more like cobblestones than teeth—brown and gritty. "You're a bloody Yank. Yanks lie. They always lie."

Miguel shook his head.

"A bloody Yank. You don't much look like a Yank, but you act like one. Yes, I can see that." He laughed again.

Miguel helped him put on a shirt. "You need some help walking down the stairs?"

"No, I can manage by meself—I'm not a bloody cripple." Unable to pick up his feet, he shuffled out of the room.

Miguel locked the bathroom door after the man left. He sat on the floor and let the pine oil seep through his skin along with the smell of cigarettes. The water in the tub looked like the London rain and the man's scars were all over his hands.

« »

It had been over ten years since that summer in London. He was sitting in his apartment packing. It was cool and dark outside. He listened to the rain, and it made him think of that summer. He found himself with an old journal in his hand. He put it inside the box with the other books he was packing, but suddenly he had the urge to read it, to pay his respects to the past. The past was never over—he'd learned that. He was not afraid to read what he had written. He opened the journal and admired the handwriting. *I used to write a lot neater. I don't write well anymore.* He laughed at something he had written. It was all still there, all of it. He had written these things soon after he had left London that summer—written it so he wouldn't forget, but it was silly to have written it, since he knew now that it was not possible to forget—not that, never that summer. It was there always. Some days he reached for that summer—

After breakfast the men were in a bad mood because they were sick of porridge and because they also knew that it was time to pitch in and do chores. Sister Susana Marie liked a clean house—I didn't blame her. Sometimes, a little order was a blessing. Some washed dishes, some swept, some mopped. The house had thirty men and Sister Susana Marie divided the men up into teams. Each team was in charge of cleaning a certain room. Andrew, Tim, and I were referees during the game: most of the men preferred to fight with each other rather than get on with the business of cleaning. None of the men were young, and none of them came from a generation that believed in doing household chores. "I'm not a goddamned woman"—they'd say that a lot. If they wanted a place to sleep, they had to clean. It was an uneasy truce between the Sisters and the men, but it was a truce, and it was a better truce than they had with the rest of the world.

Once, this one guy broke a broom handle over Frank's back. I'm sure Frank said something to piss him off, but I had to intervene. I hated being the resident policeman. I let Frank stay, but I had to throw the other guy out—mostly because he threatened to keep breaking brooms over people's backs. As I showed him to the door, he warned me that if he ever caught me out on the street, he'd kill me. A week later I happened to run into him. All he did was ask me for money. Drunks have lousy memories.

The only man in the house who enjoyed cleaning was Jim Bowie. Sister Susana Marie said he was a gentleman. "His mother brought him up very pretty." It was one of the few things she and I agreed on—that and the existence of God. (It's true we were both Catholics, but if she had known my opinions, she would not have agreed with my theology, she would not even have recognized that my beliefs had any theological basis at all.) But both of us liked Jim Bowie. He was brilliant, and kind, though I never knew how "educated" he was. Sister Susana Marie assumed he was extremely educated, because he knew how to behave himself in public. I made no such assumption: I knew too many people who were "educated" but were altogether socially retarded—either that, or they just didn't give a damn about how they treated people. But Jim Bowie was kind, and he was easy to be with. Every morning, after he finished his chores, he'd sit down and write. I always wondered what he was writing, but I never asked.

After the house was clean, Tim and I planned the menu for dinner.

What we ate depended on what had been donated to us. Sometimes we took the van and collected food from the religious houses in the London area—the Jesuits had the best leftovers. Tim used to say that "we are what we eat." I took it that he meant that all of us who lived in this house were nothing more than leftovers.

We always had plenty of stale bread. We made a lot of bread pudding and custard. Sometimes we'd run water over a hard loaf of bread to soften it, then spread cheap margarine all over it. We stuck it in the oven and hoped it would taste fresh. It didn't. We made a lot of soups, and once we even had fresh tomatoes.

The men hung around and read newspapers after their chores were done. Jim Bowie often helped the other men write letters to their families. It was a rule of the house that they were all to leave by noon and could return at 4:00 P.M. for tea and biscuits. Sister Susana Marie said even the poor deserved the small touches of civility. During the time the men were gone, the co-workers were to rest, pray, and do any major chores left undone. Mostly this meant collecting food, washing windows (even though it rained every day, the Sisters had a thing for clean windows), washing sheets, de-lousing some of the men (that was always fun—Patrick especially loved that job), giving out sandwiches and clothes to non-residents, and fixing broken furniture.

For me, most afternoons meant finishing up some work for the house and then going down into the kitchen and studying Greek. The previous year, I had flunked my Biblical Greek exam, which meant that I had to re-take the exam. Every day at 3:00 I would go down into the kitchen, make some tea, and take myself through one of the lessons in the textbook. Step by step I took myself through the process of learning an ancient language I knew I would never master. I read my translations aloud, and then re-read them. For some reason, it was my favorite time of the day, even though Greek was tedious and impractical. It was a matter of discipline—and a matter of self-esteem. I was going to pass. I would do anything to pass—it had very little to do with learning Biblical Greek.

Those afternoons in the kitchen made me feel alone, but the more alone I felt, the more determined I became. I re-committed myself to becoming a priest. It was the right thing to do—I knew it was the right thing. The kitchen was small and dark, and because it was in the basement, it was away from everything. Quiet, except for the sound of my voice translating Greek into English. Translations were futile: everything was lost in the journey from one language to the next.

Father Richard sometimes visited me there. He carried his English grammar book everywhere, but he never opened it. He had no real desire to speak the Queen's language. He told me I was wasting my time trying to learn a Greek that was no longer spoken. *"Alcabo nadie habla esa idioma en los Estados Unidos. ¿A poco te va ayudar eso en el futuro?"* He'd complain to me about how we were forced to share a room with so many people. *"Y ni siquiera tenemos servilletas en esta casa. Tan corriente."* He hated not being able to live like a gentleman. Tim and I wondered what the hell he was doing here, but we wondered what the hell we were doing there, too. Sometimes, we put our money together and bought him coffee and *"servilletas."* He liked us for it. He said we were very kind.

« »

His second week at the men's home, Sister Susana Marie told Miguel it was time to paint the women's home. "It is time, and when it is time for something, you must do it."

Miguel hated painting. "I didn't come to London to paint houses," he muttered to himself, but he didn't want to argue with Susana Marie. As far as she was concerned, the volunteers were there to do what they were told. Miguel smiled, "Yes, Sister," as if he were very obedient. He wanted her to think he was passive. Obedience was a quality she valued in other people, though Miguel never saw that she developed the trait in herself. "You and Tim will paint the women's home." Miguel and Tim nodded and pretended they were happy to do anything she asked.

The two of them walked ten blocks down the street and found their way to the women's home. Sister Therese answered the door. "Miguel and Tim?"

They nodded.

"Have you had your morning tea?"

"Yes, Sister," Tim said, "but we haven't had our coffee."

"But coffee is not allowed, Tim, and you know this." She laughed as she led them up the stairs to the bedroom where they were to begin their work. She didn't walk like Sister Susana Marie. She had more respect for the floor. She enjoyed being a woman.

"Don't you ever want to eat ice cream?" Tim asked her.

"What a strange question," she said. "I don't think I think about ice cream very much. Why do you ask?"

"Because you're not allowed to eat anything that's any fun."

"Food is not supposed to be fun. Food is sustenance. Food is to eat—to make you strong in order to serve."

"But no coffee?" Tim objected.

"Coffee is a rich man's drink. Tea is cheap. The poor can afford tea. Is it such a sacrifice to live without coffee for a summer?"

"Do you like being poor?" Miguel asked.

"Yes," she smiled, "I like being poor."

"Wouldn't you like to be rich?" Tim asked.

"What a silly question—everybody wants to be rich. It takes imagination to want to be poor." She smiled at Tim. "Do you think about ice cream very much?"

"Yes," he laughed, "I think about it all the time."

She smiled. She looked at Miguel. "You are very quiet."

"No," he said, "I'm just afraid to say too much in front of nuns."

"You are a cheek," she said. "And I must now get back to work. I am afraid you and Tim are too fond of playing, but you must remember that you came here to work. If you need the ladder, it is in the next room. Lizzie is using it."

"Who's Lizzie?" Miguel asked.

"She is a co-worker like you, Miguel. Also, she is an American. You will like her, but you mustn't say too much in her presence—since she is a woman."

Miguel laughed. "I didn't say I was afraid of saying too much in front of women. I said I was afraid of saying too much in front of nuns."

"It should be the other way around, Miguel. Sister Susana Marie informed me you were studying to become a priest. You do want to become a priest, don't you?"

Miguel nodded.

She smiled. "Perhaps coffee might be arranged, but it must be kept a secret. Sister Susana Marie would not approve."

"She doesn't eat ice cream either, does she?" Tim asked.

"Yes," she said, "she eats ice cream on holidays." She walked quietly out of the room.

"They all went to the same English school," Tim said shaking his head. "None of them use contractions except when they say 'mustn't.'

They're all from India—and here they are in England working with the poor. It's all so strange—but they all sound so innocent."

"But they're not, are they?"

"That's for sure," Tim said, "especially Susana Marie."

"I wish they weren't so damned rigid." There was something angry in Miguel's voice, though he did not know it was anger.

"They have to be rigid, I think," Tim said. "How do you live poverty without any rules? To be poor, you have to have rules."

"Most of the world is poor," Miguel said, "do they have rules? The men and women who live here, they're poor, do they need rules for that?"

"That's different."

"Maybe so, but if I was going to be dirt poor, I think I'd like the comfort of the bottle."

Tim laughed. "You'll make a helluva priest."

"You think so?"

Tim laughed. He opened one of the cans of paint and stirred it. "It's the edges I hate the worst. Takes too much patience. They're bloody hell—you can do them. You'll need the ladder." Miguel went into the next room to look for it.

Lizzie stood at the top of the ladder looking very much at home on top of her platform. She was reaching for the corner with a paintbrush, wearing a pair of jeans and an old sweater, and singing a song she later taught Miguel.

She sang it sadly, but she didn't seem to be sad at all. Miguel stared and listened. She had a high-pitched, melancholy voice. She looked down at him from the ladder. "You must be Miguel."

He nodded.

"You need the ladder?"

He nodded.

"I need it, too," she said.

He shrugged his shoulders.

"Do you talk?"

He shook his head. She had long wavy hair, but not too wavy, and she looked very Irish. She pointed her paintbrush at him and sprinkled him with freckles of white paint—and laughed.

He smiled at her but could not move.

She sprinkled him with paint again, like a priest sprinkling him with holy water. She handed him the can of paint and climbed down from her ladder.

"Where you from?"

"New Mexico."

"I've been there. The desert was beautiful—nothing like it in the whole world. I've never seen such skies."

"You?"

"Chicago."

"You have a last name?"

"Cain."

"I knew you were Irish," he said, "thin lips, strong face, soft voice. Sister Therese says I shouldn't say too much when I'm around you."

"So far you've taken her advice."

He took the can of paint from her hand, dipped the paint brush into it, and sprinkled paint on her sweater.

"You've ruined my sweater."

"You shouldn't have worn it to paint."

"When's your next day off?"

≪ ≫

Andrew and Father Richard got along pretty well. It was a miracle really. Andrew was strictly Hungarian working class; Father Richard aspired to the petit bourgeoisie, though his politics were of the left. The contradiction didn't bother me—but it bothered Andrew. I knew nothing of these men who were my roommates. It was Tim who knew everything, and Tim who talked about everything. I never found out why Father Richard had come to England—I was sure he had not come to work with the poor—he had just wound up here. Andrew, too. According to Tim, Andrew had been picked up off the street by the Sisters, and they helped sober him up. He had been at the house so long that he had become a permanent co-worker. "I haven't had a bloody drink in five years," he said. He was short, had a thick Eastern-European accent, and was in his mid-fifties. He looked like Lenin, and he liked to disagree with people. Like the rest of the men, he rolled his own cigarettes. He didn't like taking baths. He would always say to me, "Why you take so many baths? Bloody Americans worry too much about how they smell. Nobody gives a bloody damn." Every time he and Susana Marie had a major disagreement, he threatened to leave the house. "I don't give a bloody fuck. Next week I go to Cairo."

Tim would laugh and ask, "What in bloody hell are you going to do in Cairo?"

"What you mean, what I going to do there? Doesn't matter. I just want to go to bloody Cairo."

Father Richard shut us all out at night. Five people in one small room was more than he could take. He just plugged in his transistor radio and listened to it with his ear plugs. I always wondered what he was listening to—what did he hear, he who could barely understand English? What did it sound like to him? Did it sound like the Greek I was studying?

Sundays were special. Morning Mass was in the living room. Father Richard enunciated every word from the book. The whole ritual seemed to be in slow motion. Because his English was poor, I was selected by Susana Marie to give the Sunday sermons. It was one of those things I did because it was asked of me. I never bothered to write them out. I used to go into the chapel on Saturday nights and think. Maybe I prayed, I don't know—I was never very good at prayer.

He looked out at the rain. "Well, I've gotten better at prayer," he thought. He'd gotten better at prayer since he'd left the priesthood. The irony wasn't lost on him. He was beginning to feel as gray as the day. The sky was on fire with rain. He wondered if the sky would ever burn with peace. In the desert where he was from, the sky was always burning. Maybe, he thought, it burned from having witnessed. "What a strange thing to think." He looked at his writing again and was happy to be lost in it.

On Sundays I'd stand in front of the men and tell stories. I figured the only way I'd get the men to listen was to make up an interesting story and make some of the men in the house the main characters. If they listened for no other reason, they listened to see if they would be in the story. Susana Marie said my stories were entertaining, but she wanted to know what they had to do with the Gospel. "Tell them to stop drinking," she'd say. But we both knew they would never stop. It was pointless.

For breakfast, we ate real eggs and fresh bread. The men loved Sundays. As far as they were concerned, going to Mass was a small price to pay for a great breakfast and an even better lunch. The Sisters cooked on Sundays—it was their turn to serve us. We had chicken and mashed potatoes, and sometimes Tim baked apple pies. The men dressed up and most of them shaved. Tim said it was like having a real family. It was as close as some of us ever got.

One Sunday, Frank got into a fight with Susana Marie. Jim Bowie tried his best to calm him down. Frank was yelling about something and Susana Marie told him to shut up. Of course, he only got angrier and yelled louder. She pulled one of his ears and told him he was acting like a child. "Behave yourself," she said.

Frank looked at her, eyes angry as hell. "Yes, Sister, No, Sister, three bags full, Sister!" He pointed his fork at her and bent it. He threw his food on the floor and walked out of the room. He packed his few belongings and left.

Tim and I found a squat where he could live. He was neither rude to us nor grateful. Susana Marie knew we were helping him, though I don't know how she found out. She asked me how he was getting on. "Fine," I said. She handed me some blankets and a box of food. "Please give this to him," she said, "but you must never tell him it came from me."

We didn't have toilet paper. Toilet paper, like coffee, was a frivolous expense. Tim and I were the toilet paper makers. We cut newspapers into squares and made neat stacks that we placed in the bathrooms. We cut out pictures of the people we didn't like and saved them for our private collection. Every time I used the bathroom, I looked through my stack and decided whose picture I would use. Mostly, I used images of Margaret Thatcher. Tim preferred the royal family. I've never looked at newspapers quite the same way since. At the very least, I sometimes think to myself that the *Wall Street Journal* has possibilities.

Most nights, after dinner, we played games. Some of the men played cards and some listened to the radio. The Sisters didn't allow television, and the only time we ever watched it was when Susana Marie borrowed one because Pope Paul VI died. She made the men watch the entire funeral. Some of us played Scrabble. Jim Bowie was the best. "It's Jim Bowie's turn," he'd say, and he would talk as he laid down his tiles. "My life was good, but something went wrong—that's fifty points." I could have stayed hours in his presence. He was a kind man. My heart was so much smaller than his.

He remembered going back to London two years later. For no particular reason he walked down Finchley Road. He had seen Jim Bowie
stumbling down the street. He had not wanted to look at him, but Jim
had asked for money—and he remembered. "Mick!" he had embraced
him. "Mick! Mick!" he kept repeating. "Would you look at me? Just look
at me. I've gone back to me old ways. Mick…"

« »

Every morning that summer Miguel and Tim would rise at 5:30
and make breakfast. It was Tim who would always wake first. "Mick,
Mick, it's time." Miguel would make his way to the bathroom still asleep
and wash his face. He sat in the bathroom until he remembered where he
was. By the time Miguel made his way to the basement where the kitchen
was, Tim was busy putting on the porridge. Miguel had been disappointed to discover that porridge was nothing more than oatmeal.
"What did you think it was?" Tim had asked.

"I don't know what I thought it was—something English."

"And are all Americans as ignorant as all that?"

"I haven't a clue as to what Americans know and don't know—I'm
not here to represent America."

Miguel, Tim, and Patrick woke up the men at 6:00 A.M. It was a
rule in the house that everyone had to rise early and eat breakfast
together. Inevitably, there was always a fight between one of the men
who refused to get up, and a co-worker who was forced to coerce him
out of bed. Tim assigned Miguel the honor of waking up Frank—the
resident complainer. "He already hates you anyway," he said. Miguel
hated the chore but made himself smile through the ordeal.

After a while he began to enjoy his daily fights with Frank. "You're
all a bunch of bloody faggots," he would yell, "Susana Marie's gestapo
henchmen. It's a curse to be Catholic, and an even worse curse to be an
American, and when I get to heaven—you bet your ass I'll get there—
I'm going to make sure I'm in charge of waking you up in the
mornings—and I'm going to feed you nothing but cold porridge."

Tim was always wide awake as he fixed breakfast. Miguel found it
annoying that someone could be so chatty at 5:30 in the morning. Miguel would listen to him sing. Once Tim suggested they do something
different for breakfast: "The men are tired of oatmeal."

"All we have is oatmeal," Miguel said.

"We could add something to it."

"Like what?"

"Raisins."

"We don't have raisins."

"What about peanuts?"

"Peanuts?"

"We have tons of peanuts." Tim said, "Do you know how we got them? Mother Theresa came to visit here once, and when she was on the plane, they gave her a packet of peanuts. She liked them, and she asked the stewardess if British Airways was interested in donating peanuts to homes for the homeless in England. Well, you know how they love celebrities. Now, every week, we get an entire bin of peanuts wrapped in cellophane that say: British Airways. Mostly, we give them out at the door with sandwiches, and sometimes we make peanut butter."

"Peanuts," Miguel said, "it's a new world food."

"What?"

"Nothing."

"Listen, let's put peanuts in the porridge."

"The men won't like it."

"The men will love it."

When they served the porridge that morning, no one said a word. Finally, Frank broke the silence. "What the bloody hell did you blokes do to the porridge?"

"Peanuts," Miguel said.

"Fuckin' peanuts in the porridge? If you can't manage to find some decent raisins, then we'd thank you to leave everything well enough alone. If you need to get rid of the peanuts, then you can shove them up your bloody American ass."

"Don't be hateful," Tim said.

"He's always hateful," one of the other men said.

"Let 'em be," another one said.

"I ain't here to be a gentleman," Frank said, "and I don't like bloody peanuts in my porridge. Shove them up your ass—your American ass. You'd like that, I think. Americans are bloody faggots—they like things up their asses."

"That's enough, Frank," Tim said.

Miguel smiled and stared at Frank. "Some Americans do like things up their asses, Frank, but they're mostly Americans of British descent."

The Irishmen laughed. "Good on you, chap."

Frank stared at the men who'd spoken. "Long live the British Empire!"

"What the fuck has the Empire ever done for you?"

"Send the peanuts to the Queen," one yelled, "tell her Frank sent 'em."

Frank got up from the table and walked out the door. "I won't be doin' me chores this mornin'," he said.

« »

I remember Lizzie touching me. I remember her thin lips and her voice, because she was soft and everything else seemed so sad or so violent. I was lost and I had no reason to be lost, but that didn't change anything. The neighborhoods were bad and the men were broken. At the women's home, it was worse because the alcoholic down-and-out women who carried all their belongings in their bags and searched for more possessions in garbage cans seemed so much sadder to me than the men. Of course, it wasn't sadder, but it seemed sadder. Susana Marie said, "In India, people are not rich enough to be alcoholics." I would think about that. I would stare at the crucifixes in the men's home where the Sisters wrote "I thirst" beneath the image of the crucified Christ because they said they served the thirsty God. I thought to myself that here in London, where there was so much rain, I was never so thirsty. I talked about that with Lizzie, and she just nodded.

That was a long time ago, he thought, a lifetime. I'm not even the same man. It happened to someone else. I don't even remember crying about anything that summer—I was too stupid to cry—too stupid and too confused, and I didn't even know. I didn't know anything. He almost hated the young man who had written this, and yet he was drawn to him. "It was me," he kept saying to himself, "it was me."

Once, Lizzie told me about Eva, whom she loved because she liked to dance. "She's crazy," Lizzie said. "She was crying, and I couldn't figure out why." I told her we should take a walk and I took her hand. We walked all the way to the West End without saying a word. When we got to Picadilly Circus, a Londoner was complaining to a friend that London had gone to hell. "Gone to hell," she said, "nothing but bloody foreigners. Indians and Arabs, and all sorts of rubbish from the world."

Lizzie asked, "Did you hear that? They wanted the world, the British. They wanted the whole damned world. But now when the world is at their doorstep, they don't much like it. But it's too late, damn it. Now, they can keep the world. The same as America," she said, "the same as America." She said it sternly and harshly. I looked at her and wanted her anger.

I left her that night at her doorstep. She kissed me, and I wanted her never to stop kissing me. Walking home, I thought of her. I was angry. I didn't want to be in love with her. I didn't want to be in love with anyone. Love made me feel stupid and sad and empty—it made me feel like the floor beneath Sister Susana Marie's feet. I hated seeing her lips in front of me as I walked, and I hated the last lines of the poem she'd taught me, but I couldn't get it out of my head.

It was raining harder now. It was very dark. He repeated the lines from the poem to himself. He still remembered it.

He remembered that Sister Susana Marie had written to him after he had left to thank him for working there. She had informed him that Father Richard had left the priesthood and married an Englishwoman. She hadn't been very pleased, but he remembered thinking that Father Richard was at last going to conquer the English language. The day he'd received her letter, he had passed his Greek exam. Lizzie had written often at first, then less often. She had gone to law school, though he could not picture her as a lawyer. The last he had heard from her, she had married and moved to Florida. Two years after he'd left, Tim had written to him and told him Andrew had at last gone to Cairo, and that the women's home had burned to the ground. Some of the women had died, and one of the Sisters. He still remembered Tim's words: "So much for our paint job, huh, Mick?"

He looked at the pages, and thought of leaving his journal behind. Already he was taking too many books with him. He was going back to live in the desert where he was raised. It was time to go back home. Why take this with him? He turned to the very beginning of the entry about that summer in London. It wasn't a summer, he thought, London had no summer. He stared at the description of his entry into London.

Crossing the channel from Ostende to Dover, I had a dream. I don't remember anything about it, but it woke me up, and I do remember that the dream wasn't good. I was cold, so I drank too many cups of coffee, and my mind was unclear and unfocused and bothered by something. The feeling wouldn't go away. Everything I saw from the boat's foggy windows looked like a Van Gogh painting—without the passion—like his ear without his body. As the boat was reaching the white cliffs, I tried to remember the poem I'd read about this place. I knew it all once: "The sea is calm tonight"—but I couldn't get passed the first line. For some reason I couldn't remember the author's name, as if everything I had ever learned was going away. Nothing came to me, just the cliffs, but they were like everything else—gray like the rain and the salty wind, gray and thick with old age like medieval prison walls. The cliffs were like the dirty channel, grayer even than the sky, rocking my insides like a lone sweater in a washing machine. The cliffs were like the Englishman with one tooth sitting next to me, rolling cigarettes from his oval tin filled with tobacco he picked up from the streets and ashtrays and floors. I saw the seagulls flying down like mad dogs racing to pick off a piece of trash from the waters, fighting each other in flight, making the violence seem like something graceful.

I was tired and buzzing from too many cups of coffee. Everything was dim and far away and echoing, like prayers of cloistered nuns in an empty chapel. Holding my stomach, I slept all the way from Dover to Victoria Station. Half asleep, I found the Underground with its foreign distancing mumbles. I'd been in this city before, but it was still strange as if half the world had been crammed into this muggy trashcan and someone had left the lid off, just so God could hear the sounds and the rain could come in, perhaps to wash the contents: the bodies, the streets, the buildings, the stench of London's history.

I looked at the piece of paper in my hand and read the directions. I made my way to Kilbourn. A few steps away from the "way out" sign of the Underground, a woman was selling tomatoes, some perfectly red, redder than the buses, and some of them rotting and smelling very much like the man next to me on the boat.

Finchley Road was busy. It was something of a cross between a first world city—a Safeway, a Woolworth's, clothing stores, and chemists—and a third world nightmare—unshaved men peeing on themselves as they asked for a quid. The smells of a great poverty couldn't be covered up, not by the perfume the women wore, not by anything.

Queensbury Road wasn't hard to find, just a few blocks up and to the right. The neighborhood was dim like everything else, and something told me I should be afraid, afraid of the houses, afraid of this city. But I was too tired to be afraid. And the rain kept coming down, sounding like an old dog out of breath. I knocked at the door that I knew was a home for the homeless. A heavy-set Indian Sister opened the door. Her chocolate skin hid any trace of age, and I remember thinking that her white habit was the first and last and only white thing I ever saw in London. She looked at me strangely as if I were too young to be down and out, or a bit too sober and well-dressed—as if my face told her that life had not yet left its scars on me and therefore I should not be knocking at her door. "Perhaps," she said, sounding very British through her Indian accent, "you have the wrong address."

THE IDOL WORSHIPPERS

Cecilia's bedroom is filled with her past. Smells and colors are fading, every day closer to the nothingness of white. Not even the flowers on her dresser have a scent. Everything in the room smells of her old skin. On a bookshelf, she keeps books, unread, boxes filled with jewelry, and porcelain statues—antique saints she inherited from her mother. Every afternoon she dusts the bookcase, never lets any dirt accumulate on any of the belongings.

The walls are covered with pictures dedicated to the memory of herself when she was young: Cecilia is a bridesmaid at her sister's wedding; Cecilia makes her first communion; Cecilia is confirmed; Cecilia is a bride; Cecilia is a mother with a daughter on her lap. Everywhere Cecilia is dressed in white surrounded by flowers.

Above her bed, there is a picture of her husband, clear-eyed and moustached in a military uniform. Next to it hangs a picture of her parents on their wedding day: her mother is small but confident—her look is uttering directions to the photographer; her father is indifferent to the camera. The smallest picture is framed simply, a Sunday photograph of her and her sister playing in their grandfather's garden, eyes dark and wide open. The two girls have their hands extended toward something not in the picture—as if they are trying to catch something, forever reaching, forever frozen in a garden of laughter.

Cecilia rose slowly from the bed that was her home and forced herself to smile. She touched her lips with her fingers and kept them there until her lips stopped quivering. She stood as straight as she could and inhaled the stale air that smelled too much like her breath. She took in the air and held it in her lungs for as long as she could—then let it slowly out.

"I can still breathe," she said softly. She fought the pain by trying to remember the day of the week. The day would not come to her—nor the year. "You're there, I know you're there." She banged her crooked fist on her knee. "Saturday!" she said, "and it's June." It made her happy to remember.

She walked toward the window, opened the curtains, and looked out at the garden. She shook her head, biting her lip. "The grass is so pale this year." She stuck out her hands in front of her and studied the wrinkles, the thin and loosely stretched skin that hung about her gnarled knuckles. "Rotting canvas," she thought—and laughed. "I remember when the painting was new, when it was stretched tight, when everyone admired it." She laughed again. She rubbed her hands together until they turned soft and smooth. She looked in the smokey mirror of her vanity and saw the porcelain face of a woman in her twenties. She smiled for the mirror and felt herself, felt the pores, the lineless exterior, the skin she wore as a young woman, the skin everyone had wanted to touch. She reached for a gold necklace which she fingered like a rosary. Her blue eyes, dark with touches of gray, studied the reflection of the woman in the mirror and caught the images of the lovers she'd known before her marriage. She turned away from the mirror and faced the row of young men—all those young men who'd wanted to touch her, to keep her, to swallow her whole. She looked straight into the face of a nineteen-year-old youth with green eyes, the one who had been the first to get underneath. "I'm trying to remember why I didn't marry you." She tossed him a wooden smile as if it were a bone.

"You didn't want to marry anyone, remember?"

"That was 1925, Victor, and I was only sixteen. I was a little girl—of course I didn't want to marry anyone."

"It was 1926, Cecilia, your memory is going. And at sixteen you weren't the little girl you remember."

"Just because I was pretending to be a woman didn't mean I wasn't a little girl. You might have been more of a success had you realized that one small detail." She reached for his throat, but her hands moved to his collar. She straightened it for him. "You always wore such beautiful shirts, Victor." She pulled her hands away and studied the arrogant jaw, the square face that was as handsome as it was harsh. "You were a pretty man—pretty to look at, pretty to touch. You knew how to say all the right things, wear all the right clothes. I always wondered how such a poor man could afford to dress like a gentleman."

"I wasn't as poor as you thought." His eyes smiled but his lips stood perfectly still.

"You would never have married me, Victor."

"I would have married you in an instant."

"Liar."

"Cecilia, it isn't nice to call a dead man a liar."

"We did a lot of things that weren't nice, Victor—and you're not as dead as I'd like." She faced the mirror and played with her dark brown hair, shook her mane like an animal about to leap. She turned around and pointed her chin at him as though it were a rifle. "You could never tell the truth. I could have caught you with your hand in the cookie jar, cut it off, and shown it to you as you bled, and you would have told me that it wasn't your hand."

He laughed as she spoke. He stared into her dark blue eyes and touched her cheek. "You didn't love me for my honesty."

"Love, Victor? I never loved—"

"Now you're the one who's lying."

She laughed softly. "Well, it's a small lie. I only loved you a little. You were a small love. I loved certain things we did together." She broke into a bitter laugh, the memory of Victor's taste still sticking to her tongue.

"You're an old woman now, Cecilia, but life hasn't changed you very much, has it?" He reached for her hand.

As his hand touched her skin, she pulled away. "That's not true, and the worst part is that I still remember everything. Oh, I forget the days of the week, and I forget where I put things, and I even forget the names of people in photographs I keep—but what do those things matter? I still remember, Victor. A good memory is not a good thing for an old woman to have."

"It will be better when you die."

"Well, if it isn't, it's the last lie you'll ever tell. I'll scratch the green from your eyes—I swear it—and they'll never seduce anyone ever again."

"I've stopped all that nonsense."

"You stopped one woman too late."

"You're still not over that little affair, are you, my love?"

"I get annoyed when you call me 'my love.' And that little affair was with my sister, Victor. She thought you loved her. And why do you suppose she thought that?"

"She was an emotional woman."

"She trusted you."

"But it was such a little thing."

"She never said a word about it—not until she was dying. She asked to be forgiven. Why is it that the wrong people always ask to be forgiven?" She walked to the window and looked out at the garden. "Victor, the truth has a way of uttering itself. It crawls out like a worm after the rain. And all that time Sylvia suffered over that secret. It burned out the biggest piece of her. A big piece of her was ash, Victor, and it was all because she loved you—loved us both." She stared out at the pale grass. "My poor Sylvia."

"You were always such a fine actress, Cecilia. You always pretended to be so distant, so casual with Sylvia. I never dreamed she meant that much to you."

"You know nothing of me and Sylvia. I never dreamed of telling you about those I loved. I was casual and distant about everything when I was with you. I always had good instincts."

"But you never discovered our little affair. You never knew—"

"I said I had good instincts. I didn't say I was psychic—and stop calling it little. It wasn't little! Nothing you did was little. God, if I had known, I would have cut you like they cut meat at a butcher's."

Victor laughed. "No, never. You're not a killer."

"Killing you wouldn't have been murder; it would have been surgery."

"But this is all after the fact, Cecilia. When you ended it, you didn't know—and still you sent me away."

"I'll say it again: I had good instincts."

"You never bothered to explain. You owed me that."

"I owed you nothing."

"Your mother tried to cover for you."

"I'm sure she did, Victor. What did she tell you? I can just hear her: 'I'm sorry, dear Victor, but my daughter's judgment is slightly impaired; you will have to excuse her.' God, how she loved you. You were her kind of man—came from her kind of family. Her attitudes were so unimaginative. She said you came from such a 'decent family.' Decent? Decency was bred out of you along with your heart. It's quite a pedigree you come from. And she thought you were such a beautiful man. I'm surprised you didn't try to sleep with her, too."

"Don't get ugly, Cecilia."

She stuck out her hand and pointed her nails at him. "I have an arthritis that's twisted me, made me ugly—I feel ugly. *You* make me feel even uglier, dear Victor. You're a disease."

"I've changed."

She shook her head and laughed. "Gone to heaven and changed your tune, have you?"

He moved closer to her and kissed her neck. She pushed him away. "You don't believe me, do you, Cecilia?"

"What difference does it make?"

"None, I suppose." He took her hand and tried to pull her toward him.

"I won't share my bed."

His green eyes looked at her with wonder. "My God, you're beautiful."

"Yes, I was." She turned around and faced the mirror. She watched Victor fade into nothing. "Don't ever come back," she whispered. "Never come back." She felt the room turn a green hue and looked at the other young men waiting for her to speak. "Go away." They left her reluctantly—faded into the black-and-white photographs on the wall. Only her husband remained. "You go away, too, Marcos."

"Cecilia, why did you marry me? I didn't have money. I didn't have anything—and I wasn't as good as Victor." He looked toward the bed.

She rubbed her arms as if she were cold. "I didn't want money, Marcos."

"Yes, you did," he said. Cecilia showed no emotion. "You wanted to spend your adulthood exactly the same way you grew up—and that took money. Without it, you were banished from their world. But getting back at your mother was more satisfying than comfort. You stepped down to the world of the working class all on account of Mother. I was the perfect accomplice. God, how she hated me. She hated my love of working with my hands; she hated my Indian skin; and God, how she hated that I didn't admire her. We owed our entire relationship to your mother, and we never even thanked her for it."

"Irony doesn't suit you, Marcos."

His lips curved slightly upwards. His smile disturbed her. She stared at his familiar face. Her mother had thought him ugly, but she had always thought of him as handsome. Never pretty or impenetrable—natural, relaxed, and comfortable. She rubbed her arms to warm herself. Marcos was there with a shawl, and covered her with it. "Is that better?" he whispered.

She nodded. She wanted to look away but did not. They studied each other carefully.

"You know what I hated most of all, my Cecil? She treated me as though I were some kind of dignitary. 'This is my wonderful son-in-law,' she'd tell her friends when we visited her; and then she'd smile as if she enjoyed the penance. She loved the pretense of perfection. She never said an ugly word to me—not once. No, that would have ruined everything. She suffered quietly." He laughed. "Maybe she felt her silence would get her into heaven. She burned in all that silence. And you knew all that, didn't you, my Cecil? You were so smart. You knew your mother so well—so well."

"I'd forgotten how cruel you could be."

"I was never cruel."

She bit her lip. "No, you were never cruel. I loved you, Marcos. You make everything sound so distasteful."

"And you make it all sound so pure. Strange that your memory should have become so romantic. I don't say you didn't love me, Cecilia, but I do say you had greater passions."

"Don't be so sure, Marcos. We had a good life, you and I—a good life—and we learned to be silent together. It was so lovely: like monks whispering their songs. Remember?"

"Mostly your silences were like impenetrable monastic walls." Marcos played with his wedding band and looked out at the summer lawn. "The grass is so pale this year," he whispered. They were quiet for a long time. "But Cecilia," he said finally, "you didn't marry stupid—you married smart—you married a man who worshipped you." He laughed at himself and started to sit on the edge of the bed.

"Don't sit on my bed," she commanded. *"That's my bed! Mine, Marcos."*

He stared at her. "It was always yours—even when you shared it with me."

Cecilia dropped her gold necklace to the floor. She took a puff from her cigarette and frowned at the hot bitterness at the roof of her mouth.

She heard her daughter's voice as she shouted at her husband in the next room: "I can't stand living in this house with you anymore. I hate being your wife."

"If it's any consolation, I hate being your husband." The sound of their shouts bounced off the walls leaving the echo in her room. Their words lifted into the air of Cecilia's room like smoke from a fire.

Cecilia listened to the angry voices and shook her head. "Even a deaf woman could hear them. They're addicted to fighting. Death, that's what they live: death. If they didn't provide me with a place to live, I'd buy a gun and shoot them both. All I want is some peace before I die. Just a little peace, Marcos."

"What would you do with a little peace?"

"I'd think. I might even learn to pray."

Marcos shook his head. "Reflection is a fine tool for the young, but think about your life when you're old, Cecilia, and anger will start growing at the back of your mouth—you'll never get the taste out. And as for prayer, it will never happen. It's much too late for religious conversion—you don't have what it takes. You're like your mother: you like to display your dust-free statues, but they're only possessions. You're too old to start wearing religion like a piece of jewelry. The jewels don't become you at your age."

She looked at her husband sharply. "I never liked your piety."

"You never understood believers."

She held back her laughter. "Tell me, Marcos, what did you pray for all those Sundays when you took me to Mass?"

He looked down at the floor.

"You won't like the answer."

"Try me."

"I prayed to stop loving you."

Cecilia stiffened her neck. "And were your prayers answered?"

Marcos reached for her hand.

She turned away from him and stared out the window. In the next room, her daughter was still fighting with her husband. The argument was the same as yesterday's. "That's the fourth time this month he's threatened to leave her. I have nothing better to do with my time than to keep count." She didn't look at Marcos as she spoke to him but kept looking out the window at the grass. "Why doesn't he go? He's a fool, a damn fool to put up with that woman. Anger—that's all they know—anger—

all they drag out of each other. I've got more than half my body in a grave and I'm more alive than either of them. I can't stand listening to their misery anymore. Passionless misery, they don't hunger for anything. Why didn't you leave me more money when you died, Marcos? And why did our daughter turn out to be such a disagreeable human being?" She looked at Marcos for an answer.

Marcos said nothing. He stared at his wife, a blankness in his black eyes.

"I gave birth once—and look what I gave birth to."

"There's more to her than what she lets you see. You, of all people, should know about that, Cecilia. I loved you most for what you never let me see."

"How could you stand it?"

"I had a good imagination."

Cecilia smiled slowly. They looked at each other for a long time. She played with the sheer curtains as she finally looked away and stared out into the garden.

"What are you looking for out there?"

"I'm looking for more green. The grass, Marcos, so pale."

"I know. It's gone, Cecilia, the green."

He looked at her, and she knew he saw everything now. She was glad, didn't care. She started to speak.

He placed his finger on her lips, stood there watching her until it was time for him to leave. As she watched him, he grew younger and younger until he was a boy. Seven. He was seven. He was perfect. She said nothing as he faded out of the room. Cecilia remembered the great silence of the sex in their bedroom, the great silence of his death.

Cecilia looked across the room at her statue of the blessed Virgin. "Was I such a bad wife?"

The statue stepped off the shelf and stood next to her. She said nothing.

"I don't like it when you don't answer my questions."

"You don't like my answers."

"That's not true."

"All right, most of the time you weren't such a good wife."

"I loved him."

"Yes, but love has so little to do with being a good wife."

"And I suppose you would have applauded me for being submissive?"

"If Marcos admired submission in women, he would have married someone else."

"What should I have done?"

"Does it matter?"

"Tell me anyway."

"Was he a mule that you always dangled a carrot in front of him?"

"My husband was in love with what he couldn't have."

"Your husband was in love with you."

Cecilia played with a cigarette. She smiled at the Virgin. "Was your husband like Marcos?"

"In some ways."

"Which ways?"

"The walls have ears, Cecilia."

"Don't tell me you're afraid of all those men who have all that power up there in the clouds."

"Men have never frightened me. I think it's something you don't understand."

"Men have never frightened me either."

"They terrified you."

Cecilia lit her cigarette. "Is it true you never had sex?"

"Is this an interview?"

"Tell me, why won't you tell me?"

"My husband was like Marcos in that he had a good imagination."

Cecilia laughed as she released the smoke from her lungs. "I don't suppose you ever smoked?" She stared at the woman before her. She wanted to touch her, but was afraid. "You're lucky," she said finally.

"Lucky? In what way?"

"I'd trade in my daughter for your son in an instant."

"You'd only be exchanging one form of pain for another. Motherhood is a great equalizer."

"I'd prefer your pain any day."

"Other people's pain always seems so much more redemptive."

"My pain is contemptible to me. Take it. Take it."

"In exchange for what?"

"I thought you were above bartering."

"Everything is a trade-off."

"Take it."

The Virgin sat on Cecilia's bed. Cecilia moved close to her, closer until they touched.

"Soon," the Virgin whispered.

Cecilia placed her head on the Virgin's lap. "Did my mother speak to you often?"

"Sometimes."

"What did she say?"

"She worried about you." The Virgin rocked her in her arms.

"Did she love me?"

There was no answer. She found herself lying alone on her bed staring at her twisted hands.

Her daughter walked into the room and stared at her mother on the bed. "Were you talking to someone, Mama?"

"Yes. I was talking to someone."

Carmen sat down on the chair next to the bed. "But there isn't anyone in here, Mama."

"That's what you think, Carmen, the room is crawling with visitors."

"Mama, you've got to stop all of this—"

"Oh, Carmen, you stop it. You sound like my first piano teacher. I'm anything but crazy, believe me. So I talk to people you can't see. What makes you think you can see everything? You can't even see the man you married."

"Mama, no one's here. End of discussion. I want you to go see a doctor."

"Why don't you just send me to a priest to get exorcised? That would be cheaper."

"Mama—"

"Oh, what do I care what you think? Why should I care what my lunatic daughter thinks?"

"Lunatic? I'm not the one who talks to people who aren't even present."

"It's sane to argue with the dead, Carmen—the most natural thing in the world. But it's absolutely crazy to yell at a husband day in and day out. You think I don't hear? And I heard that comment about my being senile, Carmen, and I didn't appreciate it."

"I'm sorry if you heard that, Mama, but that's what you get for eavesdropping."

"Eavesdropping? The whole neighborhood heard. The trees heard, the birds, the dying grass. My God, woman, you fill this house with unhappiness."

"It's not me who fills this house with misery, Mama, it's him."

"No, it is not him—it's you. Carmen, I know you. You've made that man miserable since the day you married him. Why do you find it necessary to test him? Why do you find it so difficult to love anyone?"

"Because I take after my mother."

"I'm dying and you talk to me like that."

"Mama, if there's one thing you're not, it's defenseless. The first thing your arthritis affected was your heart—it paralyzed it immediately. But one thing it hasn't affected is your tongue."

"You're a cruel bitch, Carmen."

Carmen pressed her lips together and gave her mother a tight smile. She got up from her chair, picked up her mother's cigarettes and lit one. "Yes, Mama, I'm cruel. Cruelty is a virtue in a fight."

"And you like to fight, don't you my daughter?" She rubbed her knuckles with one of her fingers but did not wince from the pain. "I wish you had turned out more like your father. Instead you turned out more like me—but even more like your grandmother."

"Your mother was a saint, Mama."

"A saint? What category of saint do you suppose she belonged to? We have to throw out virgin and martyr. We also have to throw out mystic—"

"Mother, stop picking on the dead."

"I wish she *were* dead."

Carmen shook her head. "I don't understand you, Mama. I really don't. Grandma was one of the most remarkable women I ever knew."

"Do you know why you think that? You only think that because you only knew her as your grandmother. All grandmothers are saints, don't you know? Ask your sons, they'll tell you what a saint I am. Being a grandmother is easy—even I can do that. But a decent human being— that's a different thing altogether."

"I suppose you put yourself in that category?"

"I most certainly do not, but I at least have a quality my mother never had: honesty. My mother never acknowledged what kind of person she was. She didn't have the guts. She was a selfish, cruel woman—as cruel as you—crueler—and she did it with a smile—"

"It doesn't matter what you think or say about me, Mama, but I do care what you say about Grandma. I don't want to hear you talk about her like that."

"I don't much care. Did you know your grandmother hated your father?"

"That's a lie."

"Oh no, it isn't. And do you know why? Because he was born in Mexico, and a peon to boot. That kind of man to your lovely grandmother was good for breeding with his own kind of pauper—good for hiring to keep the garden and picking fruit. She didn't like Latins, she didn't like Jews, she didn't like blacks, and she didn't like women who enjoyed sex. Can you imagine the horror she must have felt when she imagined me sleeping with your father?"

"You're disgusting, Mother—and you're a liar—I hate you for saying those things. They're all lies, cheap disgusting lies! Now that she's been dead for fifteen years, you say all those awful things—" The tears welled up in her eyes. "She gave you all those saints—she loved them so much."

"Yes, she loved those statues, adored them every day. Did you know that she paid her husband to disappear? One day he left and didn't come back. Got rid of her husband but kept the statues. But I won't go into that story—that one would take a long time to tell."

"Stop it!"

"Poor Carmen," she whispered, "crying for the breaking image of her grandmother. Well, it's something to mourn. It really is very sad."

"You're a vicious, ugly woman."

"Carmen, stop it! You're too old to be lied to. The mere mention of your grandmother makes you behave like a child. Stop stammering. Every time you hear something you don't like, you either yell or cry. It's not very attractive. Your grandmother made our lives miserable, and that's the damn truth. It would take a few years to recount all the mean-spirited things she did to other people. I haven't got enough time left to recount all the ugly facts."

Carmen kept her head bowed.

"Carmen, listen to me—just listen. The things she left me—those things you can't see—those things are what fill this room. I can hardly stand the stench sometimes. And when I die, I'll leave you her statues.

She left them to me; I'll leave them to you. Will that make me good? Will that make me a saint?"

"She loved me."

"Maybe. But you were also very useful to her. She used you to get back at your father and me. When I die, you'll see her will. All the money—her entire estate—is payable to you—on my death. Do you suppose she made that arrangement merely because she adored you?"

Carmen showed no emotion. She was silent for a long while, absorbing her mother's words. "Why should she have left you her money? What did you do to earn it?"

"What did you do to earn it, Carmen?"

"You were never kind to her—never."

"I was kind enough to let her see her granddaughter whenever she wanted. It was more kindness than she deserved. You were a great consolation to her in her old age. And whether you want to believe it or not, it was I who made your relationship with my mother possible. Yes, Carmen, I think she loved you. But just remember, it takes no great virtue to love a little girl." She rose from her bed and sat on the chair. She looked into the mirror. "You know, Carmen, I'm beginning to look like your grandmother. Oh God, we are daughters forever, aren't we?"

"Isn't that the truth?" Carmen whispered. "Is it your goal in life to kill off all my gods before you die? You'll get in all your final digs, won't you?"

"Don't be stupid, Carmen, I just think it's about time you grew up. I've lived in your house for the last five years, and I've never interfered with your life. I think now I should have. You were just a little girl, Carmen, so easy for her to control. She never loved what she couldn't control."

"I don't want to hear any more, Mama, not another word."

"Damn it, you have to hear this! Don't you see? Every day you're becoming more and more like her. Look at what your callousness is doing to your family. There isn't any reason for it."

"You've always thought my husband was faultless."

"Don't be silly: he's a man. Of course he has faults."

"Oh, but you think he's so good, don't you? It really gets to you the way I treat him, doesn't it? Did it ever occur to you that he's a thoughtless, loveless man?"

"He is not loveless, Carmen. Stop trying to destroy the only thing you care about. You're about to inherit your grandmother's money. In the name of God don't inherit her habits. Do you think, Carmen, *do you think* that you can get rid of him when you get your hands on that money—the same way she got rid of my father? History repeating itself—isn't that lovely? Only she paid dearly for sending him away. She lost her two daughters' love forever. I wonder if she thought it was worth it. Money can control actions, Carmen, but it can't control the heart."

"How can you speak of heart? How can you have the gall to speak of heart?"

"Because I have one."

"You keep it well hidden."

"When I offered it to you, you stepped on it."

"Ha! What your heart wanted most was money. It really annoys you that you didn't get a cent from her."

"Would you like to know how that money was earned? Never mind, I won't spoil it for you. Sour grapes, I suppose. Yes, I would have liked to have had some money. If I'd had some money, I wouldn't have to be sitting here listening to you fight with your husband. Yes, I would have liked some money. I don't resent you for it, Carmen—not for that. It's not your fault. You had nothing to do with the arrangement."

Carmen rose from the chair, paced the room, then looked out the window. "The grass is so green this year."

Cecilia clenched her jaw. "The grass has never been paler." Her daughter looked at her without a trace of feeling. They sat in the half-lit room in an uncomfortable silence. Carmen started toward the door. "Carmen, just then you looked just like your grandmother."

"Thank you, Mama."

"It wasn't a compliment. Do you know what she did when she died? She gathered all her old friends and her sisters, and she said: 'Cecilia, my angel, I adore you.' A few minutes later she was dead. It was a tremendous show to the bitter end. Her audience was moved to tears. God, I hated her for that. Carmen, I won't die like that. I want to die alone—alone in this room."

"That's very nice. Die quietly, Mama—die alone—that way you won't have to express love to those you leave behind."

"I'm not a performer, Carmen. I won't die calling you an angel—*you're not an angel*. Never have been one, never will be one. And that, Carmen, has nothing to do with love."

Carmen glared at her mother and walked out the door. Cecilia looked over at her statue and spoke to her: "She disappears as well as the dead, don't you think?"

The statue stood perfectly still.

She lay on the bed and tried not to think of the pain. She breathed in deeply. She opened her eyes as wide as she could and stared at the ceiling. She thought of her sister, Sylvia. When they were little girls they used to stare at the ceiling together and talk about what they'd like to paint on it. "Sylvia," she whispered. She groaned from the pain. She could not will the sharpness to go away; it dug into her like thorns being pressed into her bones. She wished she knew how to transcend her body, her heart, her life. But Marcos was right: she had never learned to pray, and it was too late to learn. Now, all that was left to do was endure. She closed her eyes and took in the air from the room. A familiar odor seeped through her skin, and her eyes opened immediately. She sat up on her bed and stared at the woman who sat on the chair to her vanity. "I was wondering when you were going to make your visit, Mother."

Her mother's hair was combed perfectly. She touched her pearls as she straightened her skirt. There was no hint of feeling on her sharp face.

"Aren't you going to say hello, Mother?"

"I happened to overhear the conversation you just had with my granddaughter."

"Did you enjoy it?"

"You're repulsive, Cecilia. How could you have humiliated me like that?"

"You stopped pushing the buttons quite a long time ago, Mama."

"Well, I'm back to straighten things out."

"So exactly what are you going to do—have a talk with her?"

"I just might. I'd love to tell her about your escapades."

"Feel free. She'll think she's gone mad. She'll put herself away in a mad house."

Her mother clenched her jaw. "And stop asking my statue what I talked to her about."

"My statue, Mama, mine. You gave them to me in your will: tokens of your great affection. And stop clenching your jaw—it makes you look like a pit bull."

"You're a monster, my daughter. I gave birth to a grotesque monster."

"I prefer the term 'deformed beauty.'"

"Stop being flippant, young lady."

"I'm not young anymore. I'm an old woman. Go away, Mother."

"You'd send me away just like that?"

"Isn't that the way you sent my father away?"

"It wasn't that simple."

"No, I suppose not—you had to pay him a substantial amount of money, didn't you? You were too civilized to have had him killed, so you just paid for his disappearance. You made him disappear, Mother, now make yourself disappear. At least it's a trick I'd appreciate."

"I'm not ready to disappear. How could you have said all those things to Carmen? How could you! She adores me."

"Adored, Mama, past tense. And what does it matter?"

"Reputations always matter."

"Oh, Mother, Victoria died a long time ago. You were always such a stickler for the etiquette of your class."

"It was your class, too."

"I divorced it."

"Hah! You loved our class more than you care to admit."

"Wrong, Mama, but I'm so glad you decided to make this little visit—it reminds me how justified I am in resenting you."

"You could justify just about anything."

Cecilia smiled and straightened her robe. "Well, Mother, I must say, you're looking very clean. I should think you'd be smudged with the ashes of hell."

"I curse the day of your birth, Cecilia. I won't forgive you for any of the things you've said today, *never*."

"That's not news—you were never very good at forgiving."

"You should learn to hold your tongue. There are some things that should never be spoken of. It's not fair to speak of my past relations with other people in the presence of my granddaughter. She needs to know nothing about my husband, and nothing about how I felt about her father. And I was misrepresented: I never hated Marcos."

"Don't lie, Claudia, it's embarrassing. Of course you hated me. And why shouldn't my daughter know how you felt about me?" Marcos flashed his straight teeth at his mother-in-law, took off his hat, and bowed slightly.

"What are you doing here?" Claudia gripped her pearl necklace.

"I visit my wife on occasion. Sorry if I frightened you."

"You always had a rotten sense of timing, Marcos."

"His timing was always perfect." Cecilia laughed like a child.

Claudia stared at her son-in-law and looked him over. "You look the same. How dull."

"My skin is still dark, and my accent is still charming—if that's what you mean. Did you think I'd grow whiter in the grave?" He took out a cigar but did not light it. "You haven't changed much either, Claudia, but the pearls don't do anything for you."

"Swine never could appreciate pearls."

Marcos laughed. "I wish you had been so frank in life. I might have grown fonder of you."

"I didn't want you to grow fond of me."

"Well, you certainly had your way, Claudia." He moved toward her, kissed his mother-in-law on the cheek, and put on his hat. "Oh, and in case you were serious about paying Carmen a visit, I'd advise against it. You see, I might be forced to make a visit myself. You wouldn't want that, would you? Fatherhood has its privileges."

Claudia tightened the muscles in her neck. "So you think you've beaten me?"

"A long time ago, Claudia. A long, long time ago." He disappeared from the room as he was speaking.

"He was wonderful, don't you think so, Mother?"

Claudia straightened a loose strand of her hair and combed it back with her hand. "Did you really love that man?"

"Unfortunately, I didn't love him enough."

"I take back what I said on my death bed."

"Good, Mother, that will make my death much easier."

"Grandma, who are you talking to?" Cecilia's grandson looked around the empty room and seemed confused. Cecilia stared at the chair where her mother had been sitting.

"I was talking to my mother."

"But there's no one here, Grandma."

"She doesn't have to be here for me to talk to her, Nicolas." She laughed and put her arms out. "Come here and help your grandmother." Nicolas walked up to her and helped her stand on her feet. "Oh my, you're such a strong young man. I adore you, my Nicolas."

He smiled. "I love you, Grandma, I love you." He began to cry.

"Oh, Nicolas, what's the matter, my darling?"

The boy dug his face into his grandmother's stomach and sobbed.

"Come, let's sit down," she said quietly.

They sat on the edge of the bed, and she placed his face in her hands. "Nicolas, tell Grandma what's wrong." She wiped his tears.

"Mama says you're mean. She was talking to Dad, and she said you were mean."

"Well, your mother's right."

"But you're not mean, Grandma, it's Mama who's mean."

"Nicolas, that's not true."

"She's always yelling at everybody."

"But Nicolas, that doesn't mean that your mother's a mean person—she just gets angry, that's all."

"But you never yell like her."

"I do sometimes. I used to yell at your mother all the time."

"Why?"

"Because she made me angry. It doesn't mean anything, Nicolas, do you understand?"

"No, I guess not."

She wrapped her arms around him. "Oh, my wonderful Nicolas, you're so honest. You're just like your grandfather. He would be so proud of you."

He smiled, took a deep breath, and wiped his face. He kissed her on the cheek. "Will you come live with me when I get married?"

"No, Nicolas, I don't think so. But I promise you I'll come and visit you often." She let go of him. "Now run along and tell your mother you love her. I think she'd like that. Will you do that for me?"

Nicolas smiled, nodded, and ran out the door. Cecilia took hold of the Virgin's hand who was now standing next to her. She took down the picture of her sister and looked at it for a long time. "The grass was so green then," she whispered. She wanted to climb inside the Virgin's womb. "Will I see my sister?" she asked. The Virgin placed her arms around her and kissed her forehead.

"Come and hold me. I don't want to sleep alone tonight." She lay down in her bed, the Virgin holding her in her arms. She fell asleep dreaming of her sister. They were playing in a garden and the sun was full of summer.

In the morning, Carmen walked into the room and found her

mother had stopped dreaming. She was clutching the statue of the Virgin in her arms. She looked at the picture lying next to her and saw the image of two little girls frozen in laughter, forever happy. She walked to the window, opened it, and stared out into the garden. "Mother, you were right, the grass is paler this year." She kissed her on the lips, and carried the statue of the Virgin out of the room.

HOLY WEEK

"Mundo, what's going to happen after this?" Her black eyes searched her brother's face.

"After what?"

"After he dies."

"Nothing. You'll go back to Corpus Christi—to your family, your kids. I'll go back to Santa Fe, back to my work. What will be so different?"

"What will be different, Mundo, is that we won't have a father anymore."

"We never had a father, Dolores—I don't know what makes you think we ever did."

"After all these years, Mundo, and you're still angry at the whole damn world."

"Not at the whole damn world, Dolores, just at him."

"Is that all you have to give him—anger?"

"It's the only gift he deserves."

"Gift? You call it a gift?"

"It's a gift when it's all you have to give."

"You just can't bring yourself to forgive him, can you?"

"I'm not a priest, Dolores, let him look for absolution in the confessional."

"You're his son."

"Goddamn it!" He threw his cigarettes across the room. "Will you listen to what you sound like? You sound like a lawyer defending the reputation of a well-known criminal. Dolores, give it up—your client is guilty as hell."

"Guilty of what? Of being a bad father?"

"The accused has committed more than one offense."

"And I suppose, Mundo, that you picture yourself as the star witness for the prosecution."

"You bet your ass I do."

"You can be a real bastard, Mundo. I could hate you for what you're saying."

Mundo smiled at her, his even teeth shining in the light of the kitchen. "No, you couldn't," he said quietly, "you're much too forgiving, too much like Mom to bring yourself to hate anyone—especially me."

"I can't stand your attitude, Mundo. Something about your jaw—the way it sticks out when you say things—makes me want to belt you."

He smiled. "Well, I'm your brother. Sisters are supposed to feel like belting their brothers. We're stuck with each other."

"And he's your father—we're all stuck."

"No!" Mundo's whole face tightened into a grimace. "No, Dolores! No! He's the man who married my mother—nothing more. But me, Dolores, I'm your brother, not just your father's son—your brother. I'm your always friend, remember?"

She looked down at the floor.

Mundo lifted her chin with his forefinger. "Listen, I've always loved you. I don't mind saying it—I could say it forever." He moved his hand away from her face. "But not even you can make me forgive him."

Dolores shook her head. "Mundo, he couldn't have hurt you so much that you want him to die. You'd pray for his death?"

"I wouldn't pray for him at all, Dolores. His life has nothing to do with mine, and it hasn't for the last eleven years. And even before that. I never knew any kind of peace until I was out of his house."

"If you ask me, Mundo, you still don't know any peace. Not even close."

Mundo threw his hands up in the air and laughed. "Maybe I don't. But that's another story."

"Mundo, he's an old man—alone. He called us, called for you, too. Doesn't that mean anything?"

"It means you gave him my phone number."

"He wanted you to be here, damn it!"

"And I came, didn't I? As soon as he called me, I came. I hopped in my car and drove down the freeway—fast as I could. And I'll stay here until he dies. If it makes him feel better to have us around him, if it makes him feel he's surrounded by his loving children, then it's OK by me. If nothing else, I can keep you company while we wait."

"That's very considerate, Mundo. And what about him?"

"I'm sure God will take care of everything."

"But will He take care of you?"

"That's up to Him."

Dolores shook her head half laughing, half groaning with disgust. "I can't believe you'd let him die so unloved."

"You love him, don't you?"

"Can't you stop being a hurt little boy long enough to see him just as an old man who's suffering?"

"Suffering? You say, 'suffering'? Dolores, it's damn hard to feel pity for a man who inflicted so much *suffering* on those of us who knew him best."

"If you saw him, the pain he's in!"

"An emotional appeal for humanitarian reasons. Is that where this is headed?"

"I could choke you, Mundo. He's got a heart, you know, just like you."

"I think our hearts are very different."

"A heart is a heart, Mundo."

"You'd have to cut his open to prove it. What if you discovered there was only a stone there?"

"What if yours is a stone?"

"Only the part of it that belongs to my father."

"Mundo, can't you—"

"I'm not taking anything away from him, Dolores. I've never imagined his life was very easy for him, just as I don't imagine his dying is easy. So what? You think the fact that he's lying in a hospital bed, 'suffering' as you put it, excuses him from the past? He's accountable. Too late, Dolores. His cross is self-made. Let him hang on it. You can play the role of the good thief if you want—I'll be the bad thief. I don't believe."

Her eyes were growing as angry as his. A part of her wanted to agree with him, the part of her she kept locked up. She stopped herself from thinking anything at all. She heard the phone ring; she walked over and picked it up. She hoped it would be her husband. She heard the voice and smiled: "I'm glad you called ... I saw him this morning ... yes. Yes ... He got in about an hour ago ... I'll be sure and tell him ... I'm mad at him right now. I could choke him …" She looked over at her brother and grinned. Mundo laughed out loud. "Yes, I want you to come to the funeral … I don't know … I don't think he'll hold out the week …" She shook, trying to hold back the tears. "I know. Yes, I'll call you … OK … No, no, I'm fine for money … I love you, too … and I miss you … Yes, I'll call tomorrow…"

Mundo listened to his sister talking to her husband. He saw so much of his mother in her, so much of Angelica.

Dolores hung up the phone and put her hand on her temple. Mundo looked at her working hands—they seemed so soft.

"Headache?" he asked her.

"Heartache," she laughed. "Shit!"

"You're a good woman, Sis. A good mother, a good wife. A good daughter, too."

She smiled at her brother. "Why can't you be a good son?"

«Monday»

Mundo took Dolores to morning Mass. "You always go to daily Mass?" he asked her.

"Yes," she said, "I got into the habit a few years back."

"Good for you." He drove into the parking lot of the church. "It's been a long time since I've been to church."

"I figured as much. You still remember when to stand and when to kneel?"

"Don't be silly, Dolores. Some things you never forget."

In the church, Mundo watched his sister pray. There were people scattered throughout the church, all of them sitting far away except Dolores. The church was cool, almost cold, but it was warm next to his sister. When Mass began, he didn't pay attention to anything except his sister's breathing and her moving lips. She looked at home in this place, as if they had designed it with her in mind. As he sat there, his memory was thrown back to other days, days when his mother had been sitting next to him, days when he and his brother kicked each other under the pews. He remembered his father's face, his brother's screams.

After Mass, Dolores lit a candle and knelt in front of the statue of St. Joseph. Mundo stood behind her and bowed his head out of respect for his sister. She lit a second candle and lingered awhile longer. "That one's for you," she said.

Mundo looked at the small, burning candle. "Let's hope it stays lit."

They drove to the hospital without speaking. He could see the newly built hospital at the edge of the desert in the distance. He thought of his mother who had died in the old county hospital. At least his father was dying in a different place than his mother. He had once been taught that hospitals were places of healing, but the illusion had not survived.

They waited for the elevator in silence. When the elevator stopped and they both stepped in, Dolores' heart began to beat faster. *Please don't let them fight*, she whispered, "Mundo, try."

Mundo took a deep breath before he walked into the room.

The old man was asleep. "He looks dead already," he whispered to Dolores. She ignored him and sat next to her father.

"Papa, wake up," she whispered. The old man did not move. It's too late, she thought. She took her father's hand and willed him to wake up. He groaned from somewhere far away, but did not open his eyes.

Mundo watched his sister look at his father. *Her father,* he thought. He tried not to look at him. He looked so old, not at all like the man he remembered. *He can't hit me now.* He stared at the tubes and the machine next to his bed; stared at the clear liquid that was keeping him alive, a tenuous thread, fragile like a string in the web of a spider. Easy to sweep away. The old man kept moaning—horrible, unsettling groans that spoke of fear, of night. Mundo winced, an uncontrollable reaction. He wanted to plug his ears, did not want to hear that awful music coming from inside his father.

Dolores and Mundo spent most of the day in their father's room, but he never woke from his sleep. They listened to his groans, to his whispers, to his labored breathing. *He's going away,* Dolores thought. *Not yet, Papa, please, not yet.*

Mundo, staring at his father and wanting desperately to light a cigarette, shook his head. *Doesn't even know we're here, just like when we were kids.* Just like old times. But Mundo couldn't keep his eyes off the old man.

Before they left the hospital that evening, Dolores placed a small crucifix on the nightstand—that, and the rosary that once belonged to her mother. Mundo could almost see the rosary in his mother's hands. He pictured it swaying in the breeze like a swing he wanted to ride toward God. He could almost hear his mother whispering prayers for her husband.

« Tuesday »

Mundo walked out into the desert and tried to remember why he
had ever loved it. As a child he had played here, wandered through it, a
sandbox that had given him comfort, that had held him as if he were sand
itself. His mother had warned him that something was going to happen
to him out there, but he had never been afraid. He used to believe God
lived there. He remembered his grandmother's voice and her stories
about the desert: "There's a grain of sand in this desert for every person
who's ever lived. This desert will outlive all the wars of man…." He
couldn't find her voice here anymore. He tried to remember what all this
nothing had meant to him. *Jesus, there's nothing here—nothing—just
this damned dirt, and weeds, and that hungry sky that wants to swallow
everything. That's what it's done, it's swallowed everything.*

He walked through the arroyos where he once played soldier with
his brother, Javier. He came across broken beer bottles and empty shells.
He glanced at a crumpled rubber decaying in dry sperm. He could see the
hospital from where he stood, and it, too, seemed a part of the desert.
His father was there, in one of the many rooms.

He met Dolores back at the hospital. She was holding the old man's
hand when he walked in. He said nothing as he glanced toward his
father. He took a chair across the room. His father looked at him. "How
long has it been since you've been to Las Cruces?"

"About eleven years—almost twelve."

"That long?"

"Eleven years isn't so long."

Dolores glared at her brother.

"At least it doesn't seem that long."

"It seems longer than that to me," the old man said. He cleared his
throat. Dolores handed him a glass of water, and as he reached for it, his
hands shook. Dolores helped him steady the glass. "I can manage. It
takes me some time *pero siempre puedo.*" He looked back over at his son.
"You never called me."

"I called on Father's Day and on your birthday," he said stiffly. He
didn't tell him that the only reason he called was to make Dolores happy.
When did you call me?

"It wasn't enough." He was weak but still fighting.

Sue me. Mundo looked at his father and wanted to scream at him. *Just die, and don't ask any more questions.*

"I'm sorry." Mundo bit the bottom of his lip and popped his knuckles.

"You left me. When your brother died, you left me."

Dolores held her breath, willed her brother to say something nice. *He's begging you, Mundo.*

"You left me, too. Long before that."

"He didn't mean that, Dad." Dolores glanced at Mundo—*Don't.*

The old man stared at his son. "You still smoke?"

Mundo nodded.

"Will you give me a cigarette? I could use one."

"Pop," Dolores said, "you shouldn't."

He smiled at his daughter, then laughed quietly. "What difference does it make?"

Mundo handed him a cigarette from his pack and struck a match for him.

The old man took a long drag from the cigarette, then smiled. "Do you remember the first time I caught you smoking?"

Mundo nodded. "You beat the shit out of me."

"I'd do it again."

"I know you would."

"I didn't want you to smoke."

"I didn't want you to drink."

"Neither did your mother and sister—but they never treated me like this."

"I'm not my mother—not my sister, either." Mundo lit a cigarette. "I'm just like my old man—hard, damn hard."

The old man played with his cigarette, twirled it around slowly between his shaking fingers. "So why did you come?"

"You asked me to come."

"That's not the reason."

"I came," he took a long drag from his cigarette, "I came to make sure."

"To make sure you hated me?"

"To make sure you were really dying."

Dolores pleaded with Mundo. Her eyes shot at him: *Please stop, stop it, stop it.*

"Come to dance on my grave, have you?" The old man's stare turned cold.

"I don't know how to dance—it's one thing I never learned in the house I grew up in."

"You really hate, don't you? That's a lot of hate for one man. A lot of hate."

Mundo didn't answer. He sat still for a moment and looked out the window. "Nothing out there but desert."

"You used to love the desert, Mundito."

"Why do you insist on talking about the past as though it held good memories?"

"Don't you have any?"

"I had a mother who loved me, a wonderful mother. She died too young—and I had a brother who died too young. I had a sister who took care of me."

"And me?"

"Well, yes, there's you. Too many memories of *you*, Pop. The ones of you make me so sad that I could cry you a river—and then drown you in it."

The old man said nothing. He stared at the tubes in his arms. "They feed me through these things—I can't hold anything down."

Mundo looked out the window.

"I can't sleep at night. The pain—it's like someone's taking a hammer to me. Mundo, look at me. I can't change the past—"

Mundo kept staring out the window. "I can't change the past, either. I'm just one of the victims, Pop. Maybe we both are—it's the only thing we have in common."

The old man threw his cigarette across the room toward Mundo. It fell on the floor just short of him. He was too weak to hit his target. "I'll bet you'd like to use my face for an ashtray, wouldn't you, old man?"

"Mundo, get out!" Dolores yelled, "Get out, get out!" She opened her mouth again to repeat it: "Get—"

"Sorry," he whispered, "really sorry—I can't—"

"Just leave, Mundo," she said softly.

He left his sister in the room—crying on her father's shoulder.

When Dolores walked into the kitchen of the house they'd grown up in, Mundo had supper on the stove. "Hungry?" he asked her. He took a bottle of wine out of the refrigerator and uncorked it. "Want some wine?"

"I'd like to break that bottle over your head—that's what I'd like."

"I've always admired that controlled tone of anger in your voice. You've had that since you were a little girl."

"How could you have said those things to your father? He's in the hospital bed—dying of cancer—and you sit there in front of him cold as marble."

"Cold as the fists he used to hit me with."

"That's not true. He never did that."

"You need some reality therapy, Dolores. Just exactly how much do you know about your father?"

"I knew enough about him to know he's not the Hitler you make him out to be. Mundo, I know he drank. I know he was never there for us when we were growing up. I know he hurt Mom—"

"Killed her."

"That's a lie!"

"No, it isn't. He killed her."

"He never laid a hand on her."

"He never hit her, if that's what you mean—he saved that for me and Javier. But he abused her, Dolores. Yes, he did. She was nothing. As far as he was concerned, she was a garbage woman, good for nothing but picking up his shit. And he stomped and stomped until there was nothing left to stomp on."

"It wasn't like that."

"It was too like that, Dolores! It was exactly like that! You're a woman. Why don't you stand up for your own sex?"

"He could be so kind, so good."

"To you, Sis, only to you. You were his goddamned princess. But the rest of us were shit! When you left, the night you got married, he got so drunk that Javier and I had to carry him home. He fought us as we tried to put him to bed. He kept saying how we would never be anything but shit. He got out a belt. I don't even know how the hell he managed to swing that damned thing around, he was so drunk. He swung that belt with everything he had and caught your brother, Javier, right across the face. He had a mark on his face for two weeks. He had to skip school for two fucking weeks so no one would know."

"He was crazy when he was drunk, we all know that, Mundo. He's sick. He's an alcoholic. He stopped drinking ten years ago, for God's sake. Gave it all up. It took a lot for him to do that. By then he had to live with the fact that he'd lost a wife and a son."

"Two sons. By then, he'd lost me, too."

She placed her hand on his shoulder and shook him gently.

He took her hand and tickled her palm like he'd done when they were children. "But I always had you."

She laughed at the memory of her younger brother who only let himself be playful when no one else was watching. She got up and walked to the sink. "Here we are," she said, "in the kitchen. We always thought the kitchen was the living room."

"That's because Dad was always sleeping it off in the living room. We just gathered in here—around Mom."

She put one hand on her brother's shoulder and rubbed his hair with the other. "*Ay, Mundo, ¿qué voy hacer contigo?* Stop fighting him."

"Dolores, listen to me." She pulled her hand away and sat on the chair opposite him. "Will you listen to me? Mom was in the hospital two weeks before she died. He never went to visit her, not one fucking time. The night she died I had to go out looking for him in all the bars. Javier and I finally found him with his friends. You know what he said? He pointed at me and said, 'There's my son, the artist,' and then he laughed. He said I'd never be good enough. What he didn't say was that he used to sell my paintings so he could buy himself more booze. We brought him home, Javier and I, remember? And you had to sober him for two days before he was even aware of the fact that his wife was dead. And you forgave him for that, didn't you? Well, that's your choice—I don't hold it against you. I wear those memories like a permanent stain of oil on a canvas." He shook his head and laughed, "Nice, huh?"

Dolores went to the cabinet and grabbed two glasses and put them on the table. She poured them both some wine. She remembered, too, remembered her First Communion party. Her father got so drunk he threw everyone out. For an instant she hated her brother for reminding her. *Nice, huh?* "Don't idealize, Mundo, I'm not always as forgiving as you think I am."

"Yes you are." He smelled the wine, but did not take a drink. "Most of the time you forgive—it's a way of life for you."

"Yes," she laughed, "I'm virtue incarnate."

"It's not that," he said quietly, "you were taught to forgive—to always forgive no matter what. You were trained, and that's how you've survived."

"And how did you escape the training?"

"I wasn't born a woman."

"I didn't know forgiveness was specific to my sex."

"It is. Men made the rules."

Dolores laughed. "Mundo, it's not too late to learn about forgiveness—it's not such a bad vice to acquire."

"Dolores, I can't. When Javier died, it was over between me and him. Pop used to beat him till he fell over—exhausted. And Javier took it. Javier loved him. I could never understand why he loved him so much. Pop beat me, too, but not like Javier. One time he beat me, took his fists to me like he was in a ring or something. And I swore I'd get a gun and blow his hands off before I ever let him do that to me again. And he tried, too, but I ran. I only came back because of Javier. Javier wouldn't leave him. Why the hell do you think Javier got into drugs? And after he died in that accident, stoned out of his mind, the old man said he was no good. I left. I said 'That's two people in this world that have let that man step all over them. There isn't going to be a third.' After Javier's funeral, I packed my bags."

"I know, Mundo, I know," she whispered, "but things aren't what they used to be. Pop's tried so hard, and he did it by himself. No one helped him—not me, not you, not anyone. He stopped drinking, took care of himself, got a good job. He even managed to buy some property. He wanted to leave us something. *Something for us*. And he's such a good grandfather, Mundo. The children adore him. He visits us all the time. If you could only see the man he has become. The man of the last ten years is good as gold, Mundo. So decent, Mundo, you've taken ten years from his life—ten of the best years of his life."

"I was nineteen when I left home—that's how many years he took from me. Nineteen of what should have been the best years of my life. He took everything, didn't even leave me one good memory." He whispered his brother's name and took a drink of wine. He drank slowly and deliberately.

They sat quietly and stared at each other. Dolores shook her head as she brushed her dark hair back with her fingers.

Mundo got up and heated the *caldillo* he'd made. He served Dolores a healthy portion. He served himself only half a bowl.

"It's good," she smiled, "you're a good cook. Better than me."

He smiled back at his older sister. "I learned watching Mom. You were too busy combing your hair."

"Well, I was always a little vain, wasn't I?"

Mundo filled up their glasses with the remaining wine. They ate the rest of their dinner in silence.

«Wednesday»

The first thing the old man said to Mundo when he walked in the hospital room was: "Don't let them put me on a respirator. Tell them to let me die." His voice was tired. It reminded Mundo of his grandmother. He didn't speak much above a whisper.

Mundo moved closer.

"I should have died a long time ago. I should have never lived this long."

Mundo said nothing, tried to pretend he did not hear.

"Does silence imply agreement?"

"Silence implies silence."

"Dolores isn't here right now, Mundo, we can fight. You can tell me exactly what you think."

"I don't want to fight—I never wanted that. I left home, remember? I left because I chose to run instead of fight. If I'd have stayed, I might have killed you one day."

"Or I might have killed you."

Mundo almost smiled. "We'll never know, will we, Pop?"

The old man almost smiled, too, but the near-smile disappeared into a grimace. He closed his eyes and groaned, *"Ay Diosito santo, ya llévame. Ya no aguanto."*

Mundo swallowed hard and looked down at the floor. He stepped into the hall and caught his father's nurse by the arm as she walked by. "Can't you give him anything for his pain?"

"There's only so much we can do, Mr. Gomez. Your father's pain is unmanageable. He's due for his pills, though. They should help a little. They'll help him sleep."

He waited for the nurse to bring the pills. He handed his father a glass of water. He couldn't hold the glass, his fingers unable to grasp. Mundo put the glass to his father's lips and slowly let the water pass to the old man's mouth.

"Steady hands," the old man said. "Artist's hands have to be steady. I've seen some of your paintings in galleries. I even bought one, once—" His voice faded.

Mundo watched him sleep, listened to him mumble: *"Angelica, Angelica, prestame tu fe."* Mundo listened to his father invoking the name of his mother. He could not take his eyes off his father and watched him settle into an uncomfortable sleep. He leaned over the old man and laid his head at the foot of the bed.

Dolores walked into the room, but Mundo was unaware of her presence. She watched them for a long time.

«*Holy Thursday*»

The old man slept all day, a disconcerting, tiring sleep. He spoke of Javier, to him. *"Javier, mijo, me puedes traer un vaso de agua? Tanta sed. Tengo tanta sed...."* Mundo sat at the edge of his father's bed. *Javier's dead, Pop, died a long time ago.* He watched Dolores stroke his forehead.

"You think he'll ever wake up again?"

"I don't know, Mundo."

"I'm glad he's going."

"Mundo!"

"Look at him, Dolores—just look at him. You want it to go on?"

"Let's not talk." There was an edge in her voice, and Mundo could tell she was frightened. She grabbed her father by the hand and started to cry. "No, no. I hated you, too, Pop. Sorry, you don't know how sorry. I hated you." She rubbed her tears into his skin. Mundo walked over to her, tried to comfort her. She pulled away. "No, we need some time, he and I."

"He can't hear."

"Yes, he can," she said.

Mundo left them and went out into the desert to walk.

«*Good Friday*»

"The wind is so calm for a Good Friday, isn't it, Mundo?"

"Yeah," he nodded. They were both thinking the same thing.

"Remember the things Mom used to cook for Lent?"

Mundo laughed. "It was gross. *Lentejas,* that awful fish. I still hate fish to this day. *Capirotada, chacales* in *chile colorado.* Awful."

"And we'd spend the whole day in church—or at least it seemed that way."

"And the wind always blew."

"Yes. And we were always so sad because it was the day that Jesus died."

"The day that Jesus died. And we couldn't watch television, and we could never go out and do anything. We'd just sit in the kitchen and listen to the wind blow."

Mundo looked away from his sister, the sound of her voice sticking to him. He felt far away from himself—removed from his own body. He didn't even feel the tears running down his face.

"Mundo, you're crying. Oh God, please—just—please, honey, I can't stand it."

Mundo wiped his eyes with his fist. He tried to keep his lips from shaking. "You always used to say that to me when we were kids: 'Honey, don't cry,' and you'd hold me like your doll." He cleared his throat, took a deep breath, opened the window to the moving car. He moved his eyes back and forth, watching both his sister and the desert as they drove to the hospital.

When they reached his room, the old man was wide awake. He was so thin his bones were sticking out from every joint, and his skin seemed to be wearing out, like wood that had been sanded down to nothing.

Mundo smiled at his father. "You want to fight today, Pop? I'll let you use my face for a punching bag if you're up to it."

He laughed a good strong laugh, but his laugh turned into a coughing spell. "Your sister told me you had a bizarre sense of humor. I don't remember you having a sense of humor at all."

"I don't remember ever seeing you laugh."

"Maybe I never did." The old man rubbed his face. "Mundo—" the quiet of his whisper filled the room. "Mundo," he began again, "have you ever been in pain? Stupid question—of course you have. You know all about that." He looked away from his son, but found he had no other place to look. He waited in silence for a long time. "I had a dream about my mountains. God, I love those mountains. Your mother loved them, too. And in my dream, we sat, she and I, held hands, and watched them. I'm going to miss my mountains."

Mundo stared at his father as he spoke. He waited for him to keep speaking, but nothing more came out of his lips. Mundo squeezed his father's hand. "I have to go do something, Pop. Will you wait? Will you wait?"

The old man nodded.

Mundo broke into a run half-way down the hall. He raced out of the building and into the car. He drove directly to an art store, bought three brushes, several tubes of paint, and the biggest sheet of watercolor paper they had in stock. He went out into the desert and looked out at the mountains. He sat and thought—not moving—paralyzed by the image of his father. Hearing his grandmother's voice, he began to work. He never once looked at the paper. He just stared at the desert mountains and let his steady hands follow the direction of his eyes.

When he had finished his work, he ran back to his father's room. It was quiet. *It's too late.* He looked at his sister quietly sitting next to her father's bed. He heard his father groan softly. He took his father's hand. "Look, Pop! Look what I brought!" He rubbed his father's hand against his. "Look, Dad, look. Can you see?"

Soledad Gomez opened his eyes and looked at his distant son. He could not hear him very well. He could see he was yelling, yet his voice was not loud. He felt his son's touch. He saw his anxious face. He tried to focus on the large piece of heavy paper his son was waving in front of him. He forced himself to wake up. It was so hard—he wanted to sleep. His son placed the paper right in front of him. It was a painting, he could see it—he could see it clearly. My mountains. He made an effort to speak. All he could manage was a groan. My mountains, he wanted to yell. He touched the image in the paper. It was warm, as warm as the touch of his son's hand.

«Holy Saturday»

"I want you to keep that painting, Dolores—take it with you."

"I can't, Mundo, it was his."

"He doesn't need it anymore. I don't need it either."

They walked through the desert and looked into the great ocean of their childhood, the playground that had once given them peace, the only water they had ever known. He looked at his sister and placed his arms around her. He let her go for a moment and squatted down near the ground. He scooped up some sand in his hands and looked up at his sister. She stood over him and watched. "He's gone back to the desert," he said, "it's a good place to rest." He dropped the fist of dirt back where it had been.

BETWEEN WORLDS

[EPILOGUE]

The players dance on the field. The ball, as white
As a full moon in the clearest night of summer,
Bullets up, noiseless as it flies. Then falls.
It is not yet dark, but no longer day. The sun begins
To falter. Yet, in this momentary light, the grass is
Burning green, haloed, luminous. The shadows
Of men ceaselessly running, reach, touch me
And then again they run. They breathe hard, each intake
Of breath a serious matter. They yell directions
To teammates in Spanish: "¡Ahora sí!" one yells
Then flips as he kicks the ball through the goal.
He lands on his feet laughing, his teeth even whiter
Than the ball. He raises his arms in the air
As if to absorb the rays of a dying sun
And trap them in himself (he will save them in his
Body to light his moments of darkness). A companion
Runs to him, jumps in his arms, yells, "¡Así, Mexico, así!"
And after the celebration, the play resumes.

Once in a playground
At school, two boys I knew were pulled from our team.
The best players, they could only watch for a week.
Their rough Spanish, an offense. "Foul ball. Play
In English." Like them, I spoke Spanish in my home,

Copied words in English on my page. Quick I learned
And soon my father's accent disappeared. English
Was mine, the language of my thought. But
Even now, the Mexico I never knew visits when I dream.
The top layer of memories' palimpsest washes clean
And what is left are prayers learned in tongues
Never to be banished.

A dark man
Whom someone called *"Bolivia"* juggles a ball
With a tap dance down the field. Like a ghost, a man
Appears, and takes the ball away. *"¡Peru!"* they yell,
"¡Peru!" He kicks the ball, effortless aim, to another,
And yells, *"¡Llevátela, Chile!"* They call each other
By native lands. They have come from another America
Distant, but here, tonight, the green grass
Is more theirs than those who planted it.

In El Paso
Caught between two countries, I played soccer on
Sunday afternoons with men who sought asylum,
Who lived crowded in homes for the poor, restless
With nothing but time for remembering. They fled
The newspaper cities of El Salvador, Guatemala,
Nicaragua, came to live and be at peace. I grew close
To one who came from there: he used to raise his arms
To shield himself when he heard familiar blades
Of helicopters. He would not speak of memories
That covered his face with the whiteness of a
Funeral pall. In those moments, though he remained
Beside me, his heart stole him away and I could not
Cross into his sacred awful country. And then
He would return.
                    He said strange things
About this country he adopted (but which never adopted
Him): "Such a rich country, and such bad streets. What
Do you do with your money?" He never understood

This America, was permanently lost. Troubled, he had
No place to go, picked up the ways of the streets, never
Spoke the truth about himself, was difficult to
Trust. He had scars, within and without, and his
Moods were dark as his eyes. He grew angry
When he drank, but I was not afraid. He
Was too hurt to hurt me.
                              At my back
A crowd is gathered. They sit on blankets, feast
On healthy foods: salads and grapes, cheese and bread.
There is a quiet joy, expectant laughter, the waiting
For Shakespeare to come alive again. Tonight
A Midsummer Night's Dream (no better setting than a
Sky soon to be burning with stars). The actors
Will adopt Elizabethan speech. The words, having crossed
Oceans of time, will enter our hearts through accents
Distinctly "American." This will seem to no one out of place.
Our minds will open for the players. We will
Take them in. Theseus and Puck will weave their spells
Upon us. Love will cross and uncross, and all will be
Well in the end. The ball flies out of bounds. It almost
Strikes my face. But quick it is gone, on the field again.
The play that will soon begin behind me, as familiar
As the play before my eyes. Neither play is mine
Yet both beckon, call me from their separate worlds,
Will never let me go. Reluctantly, I turn. The Duke
Begins his speech:
            Now, fair Hippolyta, our nuptial hour
            Draws apace. Four happy days bring in …
The players in the distant field shout on, run on
Their game continues. Their muted Spanish shouts
Mix with careful iambics. The cacophony disturbs
A man behind me: "Their games should cease. We've come
To watch a play."
                    But soon enough
Too dark to run. The light shines only on the actors.

On the field, quiet. In peace, the play continues:
As the actors word their perfect lines, I see
Latin men in shorts taking perfect leaps
On perfect blades of grass.

       In New Mexico, one summer,
I stood on Anasazi ruins. That day, the sky was so
Deep and so blue I felt I was, at last, out of
This tired century. As I touched a crumbling adobe
It was as if I had dipped my hand in waters of the
Church. This place: more full of God than any chapel I had
Ever entered. This place: kinder than the cities
Of the World. I sat in caves the ancient ones
Had dug, the walls covered with the film of their
Smoke. But there were no bones here, no broken
Bodies or blood. Some angel or god had rolled back
The stone. These tombs were empty, everywhere
Voices: "I have lived. I have lived.
I am living."
       From the opening in the stone
I could see an unpolluted earth, a canyon, more ruins
Near the stream. The sun lit them like candles. The waters
Of the stream: a hand that healed. And everything
Was green, though the air was dryer than the sand.
This was a desert. But this was not a desert. *This was*
A land that existed between times, between worlds, between
Water and drought. This was an ecotone, a place where
All borders were banished. Ruins from a disappeared
People, tourists with florescent T-shirts; desert snakes
And rats made their nests under flowering shrubs; flies
And insects that flourished only in forests landed on vines
And cacti. There were sterile sands, and there was
Topsoil, dark and rich, where rows of corn had once
Fed hungry farmers. A cholla cactus grew tall
Raising its thousand thorns to the Indian god of light,

And next to it, a ponderosa pine forever shed its
Needles. No voices yelled demanding: "Do not cross
This line that I have drawn." And no one asked,
"Why have you come? Who has brought you here?"
The wind, for reasons of its own, was pleased
To blow these seeds from somewhere—anywhere—and
Dropped them in the soil. It pleased the rain
To make the seedlings grow.

About the Author

Benjamin Alire Sáenz grew up in the desert of of southern New Mexico, deeply aware of the landscape and of his Chicano heritage. He earned an M.A. from the University of Louvain in Belgium in theology and an M.A. in creative writing from the University of Texas at El Paso. He has just finished his Ph.D. at Stanford University, where he also received a Stegner Fellowship. He has published widely in journals and magazines, and his first book of poems, *Calendar of Dust*, won the Before Columbus Foundation American Book Award in 1992. He teaches at the University of Texas at El Paso.

Design by Nick Gregoric.

Text set in Sabon,
using the KI/Composer and Linotron 202N.
Typeset by Blue Fescue Typography and Design,
Seattle, Washington.

Printed on recycled, acid-free paper
by Maple-Vail, York, Pennsylvania.